SONG OF THE ROCKIES

BOOK 2 — QUEEN OF THE ROCKIES SERIES

ANGELA BREIDENBACH

Gems Books, A division of Gems of Wisdom
Copyright © 2021 by Angela E Breidenbach, LLC
For information: angela@angelabreidenbach.com

Author: Breidenbach, Angela
Song of the Rockies, Book 2, Queen of the Rockies Series
ISBN 13: 978-0-9980847-7-0 (pbk)
ISBN-13: 978-0-9980847-6-3 (ebook)
ISBN: 978-0-9980847-9-4 (lg print)
1. Fiction 2. Historical — Romance 3. Christian—Romance
This book is a work of fiction set in a real location. Any reference to historical figures, places, or events, whether fictional or actual, is a fictional representation.

Biblical verses used in this work of fiction are taken from the (RV) Revised Version 1885 and are Public Domain.

SONG OF THE ROCKIES

CONTENTS

To Mr. Ray Sheehan—my high school choir teacher…
You opened up my world with music when I had nothing else. You
inspired the music teacher in this book because you cared about a
neglected kid. Thank you for showing me I had value and mattered.
God used your life well, affecting so many more lives besides my
own. I hope in some small way I can be like you—changing lives
throughout the length of mine.

It was an honor to be part of yours.

You're greatly missed!
~Angie

ACKNOWLEDGMENTS

Thank you to great historians who captured moments in time that curious people like me can discover.

With great appreciation for my friend, Julie Cowan, who is always and forever brainstorming story ideas with me just for fun over lunch.

Deep gratitude to the Pencildancers: Diana Brandmeyer, Jennifer Crosswhite, Liz Tolsma, and Jenny Carey. You ladies are there for me every time. Thank you for constantly supporting and pushing me to keep going for my own goals and dreams. Thank you for answering every email, praying with me, and sending me so much love when I lost my parents during this writing journey.

I wouldn't be at this place in my life without all of you in my life and supporting my career even as I struggled to finish college and write books and handle family needs. I'm not here as an author, speaker, and genealogist because I did it by myself. I'm here because all of you kept me going when it felt too hard to do it myself.

INTRODUCTION

I'm excited to share with you a fictional story that celebrates Montana's first few years of statehood! *Song of the Rockies* continues from book 1, *Queen of the Rockies*, but this time we're exploring speaking out against injustice. The people that built this amazing state come from varying backgrounds that include immigrants from countries like Ireland, China, Japan, Germany, Scotland, Sweden, and so many more...

But it wasn't just the adults that pioneered and persevered. Children from all over the country swarmed the streets of these fledgling cities. Some as abandoned orphans whose placement either didn't work out or didn't materialize were dropped at the last stop on the famous Orphan Train. Some street children orphaned because of disease, mining accidents, or severe weather disasters. And some, well, no one rightly knows. Those historic children often banded together for safety and support.

The newsies, in many cases, rose out of the gutters selling papers to buy a meal. Boys who had one particular genetic factor — the gene for survival against all odds. And then there were those that slipped between the cracks...

Every now and then, one person takes on the mantle of hope in a world that sees no value in the nameless, faceless children of the shadows. Epic change starts with one willing heart. One willing heart impassioned by God's love will create a movement. This is a story of one willing heart who was also willing to act.

CHAPTER 1

HELENA, Montana — Winter, 1890

MIRIELLE SPUN FROM THE SCHOOLROOM DOOR. "What do you mean you'll send them to military school or indenture them?" As cold as the Montana winter wind blew against the new glass windows, the heat in her blood boiled. "The newsies don't need slavery. And they certainly don't deserve the misery of military life when they haven't even had a childhood!"

"Miss Sheehan," the superintendent spoke softly. "All the town council asks is for you to help round up the boys. You're not going to —"

"Betray them?" Mirielle balled her hands at her sides. "Those boys work hard. They trust me."

He sighed. "Those boys are going to freeze to death if they don't land in more trouble first."

"They've been fine in the Shanahan stables. Albert and Calista have created spaces with cots in the stalls. I want a better home for each of them, we all do. But they outright refuse. At least they're warm and safe."

"You made my point for me, warm or not. Refusal to meet the norm means those boys can't fit into society. They're an unruly bunch and uncivilized. That madhouse they created during the Miss Snowflake Pageant was just the beginning. Running amuck like that in a ballroom."

"They were just trying to catch the kitten when —"

"It all worked out that time, but cat or no cat, it just can't continue." He swiped a handkerchief against his brow.

"Remember those boys set up the ballroom in the first place. That has to say something about their character. Store owners are hiring them for message boys and—"

"They must become productive citizens, not gutter snipes."

Mirielle shivered. Cold, yes, but confrontation always brought out a sweat in her superior.

His eyes softened, "As industrious as the newsies are at getting odd jobs to supplement their newspaper sales, the lot of them will not make it as adults without some form of discipline and an education."

"Of course. That's why Calista and I've been meeting the boys with food each day and reading lessons twice a week." What did these people think — eleven young street boys would miraculously become model citizens? They needed love and people to teach them manners, not some convenient solution to rid the streets of orphans. "For pity's sake, these are the same boys no one adopted from the Orphan Train—to rid cities back East of miscreants. All well meant then, too. Meant to rid them of a problem and dump it on other people."

"Truly, I'm not here to argue." Mr. Randolph straightened his back and dabbed his neck. "Either you help the merchants manage the mayhem or the sheriff will."

"You'd do that?" Mirielle shook her head as her eyes misted. "After all our work, gaining their trust and friendship. Isn't the goal to help those boys become solid citizens? They'll be like caged animals. Education is the answer, not punishment."

"Miss Sheehan, they're already lacking social manners. Most folks feel the newsies are living like animals. It hurts hearts to see children scavenging like that little Joey boy even if he has the leader for a brother." Mr. Randolph rolled back onto his heels. "Frankie is barely old enough to be on his own, if he's truthful about his age. How is it right that he's trying to provide for a six-year-old?"

She closed her eyes. "Of course it isn't." Mirielle opened her eyes and plead, "Can't you see separating them would devastate not only those boys, but shatter the group? Frankie has managed to keep a ragtag bunch productive. They deserve a chance with our help."

"I think they're out of chances after that last incident." He shook his head. "Boys can't be running amuck in and out of stores and hopping trollies like leap frog. Poor Mrs. Broadwater nearly lost her shopping bags and her wits when one of those boys landed in her lap the other day."

Mirielle almost laughed, but caught herself. The inconsistent trolley schedule irritated workers already. They'd be further annoyed by boys playing pranks, fun-loving or not. "Please ask the council for a little more time to educate them."

She looked around the room as Mr. Randolph deliberated. Education. Yes! Why couldn't the newsies come here?

"I'll talk to the priests and the school board about getting the newsies into a classroom."

"I can't see how that would work."

"The church believes in charity. What better place for young boys to learn discipline and the social graces than an exclusive boys' school?" But how would they manage eleven new students? Even a church has limits to their resources.

"Excuse me."

Mirielle and Mr. Randolph startled at the baritone voice.

The intruder cleared his throat and looked at Mr. Randolph. "I apologize for interrupting, but I understand you're the one to talk to about some boys placed here as boarders."

Mirielle stepped back, the attractive man ducked to get into her classroom. She wasn't a short woman. But goodness was he a tall man — with sand-colored straight hair and light blue eyes and… She swallowed back a gasp at the sight of his strong physique. What in the world? She'd seen attractive men before. Mirielle puckered her brows at the heat searing into her cheeks despite her efforts to quell it. What a goose reacting like that!

"Miss Sheehan, I'll expect an answer by end of the week. The boys are in school and settled," he held up his hand to ward off her interruption, "or they're shipped off for a more disciplined education."

Three days. She had three days to convince Frankie to convince ten other boys to start school. She already knew the argument. How would they earn enough income if they sat in a schoolroom all day? But they wouldn't have to scrounge for meals if they'd agree to boarding school. It was all-inclusive.

Mirielle swallowed a groan. Where would she get the additional funds to convince the priests and the headmaster the new school could support eleven more boarding students?

Mr. Randolph turned to the visitor. "And you, sir, are?"

The handsome man extended a hand to the school's headmaster. "Evan Russell, sir." They shook. His eyes flicked up to Mirielle's as he also offered a polite handshake to her. "Ma'am."

A tingle raced from fingertip to elbow to shoulder to heart. Mirielle's eyes grew wide at the ripple. She couldn't look away from his similarly stunned eyes. And that ripple hadn't stopped racing through her arm like a sudden flash flood rushing into her heart.

"Miss Sheehan?" Mr. Randolph broke into her silence. "I believe your duties call."

"Um, yes." She snatched her hand back. Flustered? The teacher who could manage the toughest child and go toe-to-toe with the most demanding parent? She never flustered. What did he do to her? "My—uh—pleasure to meet you, Mr. Russell." Mirielle forced herself to back away.

His gaze stayed connected to hers as Mirielle bumped into her desk and then felt her way around it like a miner in a blackout. A flush rushed boot to root. She jerked her chin away and plopped into her seat. Better to concentrate on grading than on being graded by a strange man. She swallowed. Such a man, for certain, with strong, wide shoulders filling out the heavy wool coat.

He seemed to hear Mirielle's thoughts as his gaze still heating her skin. Electricity passed between them as strong as the gusts against the glass.

CHAPTER 2

EVAN YANKED his attention back to the superintendent. Mining had been a long, lonely process, as he'd built up savings to provide for his son and their future. He'd come looking for Joseph, not a new wife. But even his poignant memories of pretty Nadine didn't rival this russet-haired beauty that seemed to flush at the slightest glance. If he intimidated the little school marm, how in the world did she manage a classroom of children?

"Mr. Russell?" The superintendent waited.

"I'm sorry." He mumbled to the tubby man. "I think I left my manners in the mine." It'd been a long time since he'd experienced a woman's scent, er, presence.

"Well, how can we help you, then?"

"My son is missing, sir." Miss Sheehan's inhale caught Evan off guard. He cleared his throat. It still hurt every time he had to repeat it, but sympathy choked him to silence. Do-gooders needed to either help him or stay out of it. He dredged deep for the courage to tell it one more time. "I left him with relatives after my wife died. I had to work elsewhere. For a long time, I'd get an update once a month. But those updates stopped coming a year ago. Being the dead of winter, I assumed mail was having trouble getting through. After the melt, I came over the mountains. When I inquired, I heard…" He ran a hand through his hair. "My brother's home burned down, and according to all accounts, my family was lost."

"Oh Mr. Russell, I am so sorry." Mirielle crossed herself and bowed her head.

Evan cleared his throat again. "They did not find my son among the ruins. I was directed here to ask if any families might have taken him in and registered Joseph with their children."

"Joseph, you say?" Mr. Randolph scratched his head. "We have several by that name, but all have known parents."

Evan's heart sank. Maybe it was true. Maybe Joseph didn't make it through the fire. "Is there a way to question the children? Or let me see them? Maybe one of the boys was taken in or adopted." He knew desperation tinged every word. What else could he do? Where could a little boy wander off to, with no one noticing?

"I realize the dire nature of the situation, Mr. Russell. But there's no possible way we could impose on the families of this school for a search. You're simply asking too much. We know each child here. What would you do if we found him adopted? You certainly couldn't suddenly show up and abscond with a child."

Abscond? "Not just a child, sir. My son!"

The young lady cleared her throat. "May I?" Miss Sheehan certainly didn't wait to be invited as she offered,

"What if the child weren't here, but a child here knew of him?"

Hope lit in Evan's heart. He'd have made friends. Of course!

"I do see all the children through music class each week." She rejoined the men. "If Joseph attended our school, I'd know. But, no sir, all the boys belong naturally to their parents."

The hope dimmed.

"Mr. Russell, we could send out notices to the parents. Then, if a family knows your son, they'll let us know. But I have another idea for you."

Evan's emotions jerked up and down like the backside of a bronco. "I'm listening."

"As am I, Miss Sheehan." The superintendent raised his eyebrows.

"Come with me to meet the newsies."

"The newsies?"

She held up a forefinger and tipped her head forward as if conducting an orchestra. "I know eleven little boys who would love to earn a penny or two." Her hands gracefully lowered.

The fatigue of frustration set an edge in his voice. " What makes you think a bunch of—" Evan clamped his mouth shut at the sudden fire in her eyes as Mirielle's hands pinched the air, punctuating the sign for a dramatic rest.

She gave him a direct challenge. "Do you have a better idea? They can spread out and look in places no adult would think of searching. One might think your love of a few pennies —"

"No, no. Nothing like that." Now he knew how she

managed a classroom full of boys. Could a motley cluster of newsboys fan out and find Joseph in Helena?

"You won't know until you try." She looked him straight in the eye, not a hint of falsehood in her voice. "And they're nice boys."

The superintendent added, "They are nice, if a bit unruly. But we have plans to solve that issue."

The teacher's back stiffened. "In the most loving way possible for their future success."

Miss Sheehan's voice softened as she placed fingertips on his bicep. "Are you willing to try?"

The weight of her touch soothed him even through the heavy wool of his coat. Evan nodded and concentrated on the hope she offered. He liked her optimism. Something sorely lacking in him right now. "I'll try anything."

CHAPTER 3

EVAN GLANCED across the street at the bedraggled lad on the corner of Main Street near the trolley stop. He waved a paper high in the air and sang out the headlines hawking to an oncoming crowd. Then the boy moved into the path of several businessmen.

"He's an enthusiastic salesman." Two of the men dropped coins into his palm as the newsie deftly snapped a paper, one after the other, into their hands. No one had stopped walking in the exchange, with the boy walking backwards, keeping up with the men. "Can't fault his methods." Evan chuckled. "I don't think he's going to miss one sale today."

"That's Frankie." Mirielle said as she waved to the boy, catching his attention. "He's been very successful for the paper. For himself and the boys he leads, too, but even so that's a pittance to live on."

He flapped a paper back at her in acknowledgment from his prime corner.

"Frankie is the leader of the newsies that take reading

lessons from Calista and I, after they finish catching end-of-the-day workers off the trolley." She turned to look at Evan, eyes sparkling like the sun off Montana snow, brilliant and shimmering. He could tell she loved those boys. "We'll wait here so we don't interfere."

He nodded and let his gaze roam her happy, upturned face. Joy radiated out of her like a campfire on a frosty night. This woman wasn't making a show of charity. It was as much a part of her as the speckling of freckles on her cute nose. The warmth expanded, wrapping Evan in cozy comfort, though the overcast sky hung low and the wind blew wisps of snow by their feet. He wanted to scoot closer and bask in what he'd missed for so long. If his soul had hands, they'd be reaching toward her feminine allure as if to a campfire's glow. What would it be like to be held in this woman's arms? To feel the depth of caring towards those she obviously loved?

Evan blinked away the distracting thoughts and lifted the basket he carried for Miss Sheehan. "So you bring them food twice a week with their lessons?"

She smiled. "They can't learn on an empty stomach. But we take turns with a few other women so the newsies get something every day. Today is my day. Calista and Albert feed them a small breakfast in the mornings. Then some other families help with food on different days of the week." Her simple gray dresscoat and bonnet didn't make her stand out compared to the passersby. But people seemed to know her well as she bobbed a nod here and there through their conversation.

"I don't mean to pry, but how can you supply enough food for all those lads on a teacher's salary?" Evan looked back at the boy. His clothes mismatched, dirty, with trousers too short. One out of eleven growing boys being fed by a handful of good-hearted women. Would they find Joseph learning to sell newspapers, mixed in with the industrious desperate newsies? Evan's heart picked up like an expectant drumroll. Surely Miss Sheehan would have known if an odd child showed up in the group.

"Just another minute, Miss Mirielle," Frankie called over, "and I kin whistle fer them." He handed off a paper and collected a coin from a businessman.

She cupped her hand around perfectly formed lips and called back over the street din. "We can wait." As the boy sold his last few papers, she turned the conversation back to where they'd left off. "There are a couple of shops that share day old bread and odd items. Our church runs the school. I'm able to collect any leftover food as charity for the needy. These children are the neediest of the needy."

Another trolley clattered to a stop at the corner. Frankie ran to meet it, whistling and singing out his headlines. The disembarking passengers raised the noise level in the darkening streets even as the packed snow muffled their feet.

"I don't know what we'll do if more children show up." She shrugged. " I suppose we just keep trusting as we keep on doing."

Evan leaned a little closer and spoke nearer Mirielle's ear so she could hear him over the din. "He's so confident. How old is Frankie?" He inhaled the scent of lavender and cedar. The smells of peace, comfort, and womanly softness. He hovered a tad longer. The starvation of loneliness struck him in the gut as harshly as a lack of food.

Mirielle shivered in the wind while her cheeks pinked. "Uh, around twelve or thirteen, he thinks."

"He thinks?" Evan pulled away before she had a chance to consider him a looney. "He doesn't know?"

She looked up. "He could be younger, but he tells folks as old as they'll believe so they'll leave him be." A huskiness crept into her voice. Had his nearness caused it, or was the cold affecting her throat? Evan pushed the thought away, trying to concentrate on her words rather than the sound of her voice. "Frankie's family never had money to celebrate birthdays, and then his father died in a riot for worker's rights. His mother fell ill while working a factory job and never recovered."

"He's shared all that with you?"

"Over a period of time, as I've gained his trust." Mirielle looked toward the end of the street and tipped her head in the direction of the rail yards even as she pushed her hands back into the muff. "Frankie arrived on the orphan train with his little brother last year sometime. He'd been on the city streets in New York before the authorities forced him out." A shimmer of moisture filled her eyes by the time she turned to face him again. "By the time they rounded up the street urchins to clean up their problem with vagrant children back east, Frankie was too old and streetwise for people to want to adopt him—and not quite big enough to work the farms."

As a gust of wind blew, Evan moved to block Mirielle from as much of the cold onslaught as he could. "How old do you think his little brother is, then?"

She shrugged. "I'm not sure, but possibly six."

About the same age as Joseph. Evan's son could be in the same shoes, or lack of shoes, if he didn't find him. If he was still breathing. *Lord, have you sent compassionate people to care for Joseph as you have these youngsters?*

"Heya, Miss Mirielle. Who's ya got with ya?" Frankie hopped up on the sidewalk with them.

"Frankie, this is Mr. Russell. He's here to help today with our reading lesson."

Evan hooked a wide-eyed stare over Frankie's head at Miss Mirielle. When did he say he'd help teach? "I am?"

She peeked up from under the brim of her gray winter bonnet while long pink chin ribbons flapped against her coat buttons. "You do know how to read, correct, Mr. Russell?"

"Yes, yes, I can read. I thought… well, I thought…" What exactly did he think he'd be doing when Miss Sheehan asked for help?

Frankie's eyes narrowed. "I ain't so sure the guys 'er gonna want a stranger's help. We bin hearin' stuff 'n such 'bout getting rounded up again." He gave Evan a slow study.

"Come now, Mr. Russell isn't going to round you up any more than I am. We're going to teach you how to read, so you can sell more papers, and one day get a better-paying position." She gave Frankie her best no-nonsense I-expect-your-best-effort teacher face to make her point. Then she added, "However, I do want to ask your assistance with something."

Frankie's face lost the icy suspicion. "Me and my guys would do pretty near anything to help you and Miss Calista."

"After our lesson today, Mr. Russell would like to hire your team to help him find someone. Do you think you boys would be up to that project? I think there'd be some pay in it for all of you, right, Mr. Russell?"

Evan latched onto the cue. "Frankie, my son is missing.

His name is Joseph, and he's about the same age as Miss Sheehan, here, says your little brother might be."

That suspicious look crept back over Frankie's face as stepped backward.

"I'd like to hire you and your crew to scour Helena and help me find him, if he's still here."

"How d'ya lose yer boy, Mr. Russell? That's somethin', losin' a kid out here."

"Frankie!" Miss Mirielle admonished, "He didn't do it on purpose."

Frankie looked duly chastened for a moment as he scuffed a toe at the sidewalk. Then squinted his eyes at Evan, waiting him out in silence.

"No, it's all right." Evan smiled through his own suspicions. What was it with this kid? The trust factor felt more like a ride in a runaway stagecoach. And about as subtle. "He was staying with family because his ma passed away. They're house burned down last winter and I lost my brother's family." Evan's voice thickened. "No one knew what happened to my son, though. I didn't know until I could get through the mountain pass from my stake."

Frankie stared down at the ground. "That's sure a sad thing ta have happened." He looked up, but didn't quite meet Evan's eyes, and said in a guarded tone, "Yeah, let me talk with my guys and we'll be lettin' you know."

Whistling a high-pitched signal, Frankie took off toward three other boys. He pointed to Mirielle and Evan, then rounded a building out of sight.

"Huh, wonder where he went?" Evan looked into the distance. "That boy sure can whistle."

"He just went to collect the kids further downtown. They use a series of whistles to communicate." Her hand moved to the corner of the basket. "I always bring a little sweet enticement on reading days to reward their efforts." She lifted the dishtowel, revealing red McIntosh apples, sandwiches, and cookies inside the basket. "Best students I've ever had."

Evan looked from the basket to her smiling eyes and swallowed hard. She'd be a sweet enticement enough for him to do just about anything. If she wanted him to read to boys this afternoon, that's exactly what he'd do. This sweet-hearted woman was the closest he'd come to any break-through ideas for finding Joseph. It was downright enjoy-able to see her mind spin those golden threads like a spider weaving an artistic web sparkling in the sunny dew.

He blinked away the romantic thoughts. His focus needed to be on one target—finding Joseph. Women could wait. Evan slid away to give himself lavender-free air. But Miss Mirielle's presence kept sending flickering sparks deep into Evan's gut.

CHAPTER 4

"HERE'S SOME HARD-WORKING NEWSIES, if I've ever seen one!" Mirielle laughed as she handed out nine turkey sandwiches. "But where are Joey and Ernst?"

Frankie scrunched up his lips for a moment. "We had some extra papers, so I had ta send 'em back. I'll take 'em their stuff, if that's okay."

"Of course, Frankie, but they're going to miss reading and the extra treat, too, then?" She held up a cookie. A round of oohs and ahs came from eager students. But the boys knew they had to do their lesson prior to the last reward, even one as special as a thickly frosted cookie. If only her regular students would be so easily rewarded. Her heart hurt that the newsies could count the number of cookies they'd ever had and stop before hitting all ten fingers. The children in her classes could likely count that in a matter of weeks. What one child took for granted, another held as precious treasure.

"If'n you'll let me, I'll borrow yer book and show what we done learnt today."

Mirielle dipped her head, thinking. Losing the reading book would put them weeks behind. Frankie already displayed more responsibility than most boys his age. If she showed trust, it'd be a better lesson than if she argued for her way. "Well, that sounds like a suitable compromise. Let's get situated. Where would you like to go for our lesson, boys?"

Jonathan piped up, "Miss Mirielle, we got told we could all sit in the hotel ballroom from now on when it wasn't bein' used since we took such good care of it after the last party. The manager even said we could pull out chairs if'n we's ta put 'em back when we're done."

"My goodness, that's generous. I am so impressed, boys, that you've earned such respect after the…" She cleared her throat and lifted a brow, ignoring Evan's curious eyes, "…kitten incident. Only hard work and courteous behavior earns those kind of rewards."

"We cleaned up and then went back and offered to work off our trouble. We been gittin' asked to help ever since." Frankie shrugged. "Don't think it's gonna be enough though to keep us together though. People jes don't like street kids." He dug into the sandwich.

The businessmen of this city had been offering various meeting spaces as the boys did odd jobs for them. What if those same businessmen were willing to sponsor the cost of these boys' education? With the volume of millionaires in this city, more than she could track from rich mining strikes, she could find a few supporters. If anyone could afford to donate, all those men could. Wouldn't they see an excellent investment and a future infusion into the work-force? Young boys would learn gratitude, respect, and loyalty because good men provided opportunity.

The ideas pinged around in her mind, growing with each new thought. But without discipline, none of it would work. Without trust, discipline would feel like judgment or unjust anger aimed at them from adults. That perception would feed the boys' distrust. A vicious cycle Mirielle wanted to circumvent.

Trust and discipline. Everything hinged on those two elements. What if she built both around the newsie's already strong team spirit? Something they had to learn together, rather than individually—like an orchestra. Mirielle glanced at the scruffy group. No, that would take years none of them had.

Mirielle held open her arms and gathered the boys into a group, Evan behind them. She sent him a quick nod and smile. "Listen and see what you think."

She lowered her voice to keep their attention on the importance of her words. One teaching concept that worked well in nearly any situation. The quieter she spoke, the more the boys leaned in to hear. "I've concocted a plan to keep you all together. I think I can convince everyone to go along with it." She paused, allowing their imaginations to catch onto the adventure while she plunked the food basket onto the sidewalk near her feet.

"A plan?" Frankie pressed to the front of the group.

Would they catch onto her Tom Sawyer tactics? "Oh yes. I might need a little help, though. It'll take some crafty newsies to pull it off. But if we do, yes if we do..." She took a deep breath and whistled through her teeth, mimicking the boys' signal for a grand sale.

One boy puffed his chest and proclaimed, "We can do anything, Miss Mirielle."

"I believe you can." Building the mystery and adventure,

Mirielle added, "If we pull this off, I think you boys will be the pride of Helena. I mean," she threw her arms wide and tossed her head back. "You boys will be what our town folks talk about for years to come." She leaned back into the circle. "Nobody will want you gone. They'll be begging you to stay like the hotel manager just did. The pride of Helena, they'll say." The beauty of her plan included that Mirielle wholeheartedly believed it, too.

The boys' grins spread across faces, and they buzzed questions. "What do we gotta do, Miss Mirielle?"

"Yeah, what?"

"He got somethin' ta do with it?" One boy thumbed a gesture at Evan.

Mirielle wanted to burst out laughing at Evan. He was as tuned into her as each of these young ones. All hung on her words as if she were the Pied Piper. She built to the climax. "That's the icing on the cake! Yes!" She stood up and fisted her hands on her hips.

"Ya gonna tell us? Huh?" Jonathan tugged at her sleeve.

"You bet I am." She hunkered down into a huddle, shoulder-to-shoulder, with boys crowding in closer. "We're going to do something amazing. Something extraordinary. Are you listening?"

They nodded in unison, not one of them noticing Evan any longer.

"We're going to create the Newsies Pipe and Drum Corps. You are all going to get the chance to go to school, eat three meals a day, and sleep in normal beds in a dorm. No more scrounging. No more worrying about getting shipped off to military school or forced into indenture. You boys are the future of Helena and we're going to make it happen together."

"Ooh, beds." Danny said in awe until Jonathan elbowed him. "Hey!"

"How we gonna do that?" Jonathan asked. "That's some pretty tall 'spectations."

"We're going to have some help from the men of this city." She'd sell each and every one of them on the idea. And if they told her no, well, she knew their wives and sweethearts. "Tonight, after our lesson, you boys are going to scour the city for Mr. Russell's son. He's going to pay you." She looked up at Evan for confirmation. At his nod she continued, "While you're doing that, every time you speak to another soul, you will prove you're courteous, kind, and hard-working. You hear me?"

A chorus of, "Yes ma'am" rounded the group.

"Every interaction you have with people on the street will be polite. You are now the most important salesmen Helena ever had. You are going to show the people of Helena that you're trustworthy. If you'll do your part, you'll give me the opportunity to do mine."

Frankie cocked his head, voice dripping with the collective curiosity. "What 'cha gonna do?"

"I'm going to talk till I'm blue. I'm going to get every one of you sponsors so you can go to that private school I work at, get instruments, and give you all the same opportunities that rich boys get." She stopped talking and gave each newsie direct eye-to-eye contact. "Can you give me the time to put it all together?"

"I can."

"Yep."

"I dunno if it's gonna work." Jonathan tossed into the crew. "You gonna get us all taught up ter be like him?"

Jonathan thumbed at Evan. "And playin' some kind of sissy flute instrument?"

The newsies shuffled their feet, backing up as if the plan unraveled. Mirielle's stomach twisted. What else could she do if the boys didn't want her help? They were running out of time.

Evan cleared his throat.

The boys all swung their heads around to see him.

"Pipe and drum sissy? No, sir." He shook his head. "Those men are the fiercest, bravest men on the battlefield. Without the fife, the drum, and the men brave enough to go forth, we'd have no nation. Who do you suppose kept the rest of the men marching? Who do you suppose gave courage to the battalion? As long as they could hear the music and see the flag, our forefathers refused to give up the fight. And that is why we have our freedom today, my young friends. It's thanks to the brave men that kept the battle going."

A collective "Oh," and wide eyes on each child put the plan back into play.

Jonathan asked, "So yer thinkin' we kin be like them? Brave and free?"

He pursed his lips and made a show of considering the plan while rubbing his chin. "I believe it can work. I believe enough in Miss Mirielle's plan that I'll work with her on figuring out the logistics on one condition." He lifted a finger to match his words.

"What's that?" Frankie asked.

"You boys start with me. You work hard helping me find Joseph. I'll share all I know, and I'll work hard for you in return. Might even be a sponsor if Miss Mirielle will help me understand what's all involved."

Frankie sized up Evan. "So you'd do that even if'n you gets yer boy?" The rest of the newsies watched Frankie's body language and waited. His eyes narrowed again, as they had earlier. The other boys followed suit. Frankie chewed his bottom lip. The rest of the boys worked their bottom lips.

"I would."

Then, after a gut-wrenching pause for Mirielle, Frankie nodded slowly. "Deal."

Evan stuck out a large hand, "Shake on it." He glanced around the group. "Every one of you. A man's word matters."

Frankie grabbed onto Evan's hand. They pumped twice. Frankie stood back, never breaking eye contact. "You good for yers?"

"I am. Are you?"

"I am."

"What about the rest of you?"

They lined up. Eight more boys pumped Evan's hand.

Would he really support her in the long haul as he just did here?

Then Evan turned and stuck his hand out to Mirielle. "Do we have an agreement?"

A sparkling smile spread across her face. She looked at each boy again. The anticipation pouring out of them like the smell of bacon on a Sunday morning, strong and full of rich promise. "We sure do, Mr. Russell. We sure do." They shook hands to the hoots and hollers of the newsies.

CHAPTER 5

THE LESSON ENDED. Mirielle handed out a large, heavy gingerbread cookie slathered in thick, white frosting to each student as they finished cleaning up the hotel ballroom. "Frankie, here are the extra cookies for our two missing boys.""They'll be real excited, thanks."

She put a hand on his forearm and held him with her for a moment. "But do please encourage them to come next time?" Mirielle watched as Frankie's eyes shuttered. Had the two gotten themselves into trouble and Frankie covered for them? "You know you can tell me if one of the newsies ever needs help, right?"

He looked away and busied himself with carefully wrapping a napkin around the delicacies and then tucking cookies into a coat pocket. "I know, Miss Mirielle."

Before she could dig further, Evan brushed his hands together as he joined them. "Well, that's that. Most of the boys are off to their assigned streets. Which are you going to pick, Frankie?"

The lad glanced up into the much taller, broader man's

eyes. "I'll get my other guys and we'll cover Reeder's Alley. I figure that's where lots of kids go if'n they don't got no regular spot. Lots a places to pitch a spot and not get caught."

Mirielle smiled. "You're right. Take care and I'll see you in a couple of days."

"Yes, ma'am." He ducked out of the door in a flash of gangly legs.

"He had good parents before being orphaned. I can tell he knew love."

Evan turned to Mirielle. "You amaze me." His eyes glowed with admiration. "Your faith in children no one else believes in and seeing them as no one else can. Somehow I think hiring these newsies is going to bring my son back, if it's going to happen."

If it's going to happen. Prickles slid down her spine like ice skates over the local pond—smooth and pleasing while sharpening her senses to a crack in the surface. No. She swallowed back the sudden fear. There could be no fracture in the team's purpose. Not a bit of doubt. Hopelessness sprouted as easily as faith. Whichever seed they chose to plant, that's what they'd harvest.

"Don't say that, please." She stood and faced her new friend and teammate. "We have to believe we will find Joseph. We have to instill that belief in the newsies or none of us will have the drive to push through the rough days."

HE STRAIGHTENED HIS SHOULDERS. "THANK YOU. I think God directed me to you because I needed my own belief shored up." Evan ran a hand across his heart. "I've been looking for my son for so long that it feels hopeless." *God, is this why you created woman for man? We need her to speak encouragement into our souls and help us keep fighting. I think I could fight a lifetime for her.* He shook his head as if to answer his own question. Loneliness battled with common sense. Mirielle Sheehan was a kind, God-fearing person who simply had an extraordinary empathy for lost children. The newsies were prime examples.

"It's not hopeless, Mr. Russell, it's not." Mirielle reached for his hand.

Though her touch was cool from the chill in the ballroom, when they connected, Evan soaked her essence into his heart like the dirt outside the claim sucked up the rare summer rain. He sandwiched her hand between both of his without thinking. The desire to provide warmth and comfort as instinctive as it had been toward his wife.

"Evan, please. Sorry, those boys already have me calling you Miss Mirielle."

"I like the natural way it happened. But just call me Mirielle when we're alone." She gasped and snatched her hand back. "I didn't mean—"

"I didn't take it that way." He assured her, then noticed the little flecks of gold in her eyes. They sparkled like specks in clear water, the kind that proved invaluable.

"Evan?"

"What?" He blinked.

"I asked you if we should choose a street, too."

Was she that unaware of him? Was he that distracted by her? "Let me put you in a carriage and get you home. I can keep looking."

"But I want to help."

He couldn't have her along and stay focused. "I'll cover more ground, faster, without you. I hope you understand."

She looked hurt, but grace floated around her words. "Oh. I hadn't thought of it like that. I thought if you drove your carriage, we could cover both sides of the street. One could watch both directions."

"It sounds like a good idea that might have worked the first day Joseph disappeared. But by now he'd be established doing something, wouldn't he? And what about your family? Won't they be concerned? It's getting late."

"I live at the school in my own apartments." Mirielle's voice a near whisper. "No family."

An orphan? Mirielle Sheehan is an orphan? Understanding and compassion overwhelmed him. No wonder she poured herself heart and soul into helping these boys.

"You're not letting me do this alone, are you?"

She shrugged. "I have a talent for finding lost boys." She gestured at the area around them as if all the boys still sat at her feet.

"I accept." She also seemed to have a talent for finding lost hearts. Could he be so lucky as to find his son and a woman to love? Evan's sense of hope grew a little larger. Hope, it seemed, that stemmed from the moment he'd laid eyes on one Miss Mirielle Sheehan.

CHAPTER 6

MIRIELLE PLACED an open invitation to a tea in the local
society column. "Thank you." She left the newspaper office
with a lighter step. They hadn't found Joseph last night.
But with permission from the school board this morning,
she planned a sponsorship meeting focused on finding
funding. With one confirmed sponsor already, she managed
to get another week added to the deadline for the
newsies.The tea would take place in her music room so
attendees could tour the school, see the dorm area, and
make pledges. Church, school, and town leaders would all
attend just four days from now… she hoped. That would
leave three days to avoid the newsies being rounded up and
shipped off.

Frankie swung off the back of a passing trolley and
trotted up the sidewalk to Mirielle.

"Afternoon, Frankie. Did Joey enjoy his food yesterday?"

"Oh yes, ma'am. He woofed it down faster than a dog
catchin' a stick."

Mirielle giggled at the colorful description. "And did he practice reading?"

"Yep, sure did. He said his alphabet and even got his numbers up to one hunerd. He said I was to be sure to tell ya he only messed up once on his numbers. I gave him his cookie, anyway."

"He definitely earned it then." She ruffled his hair. "Frankie, maybe you should become a teacher one day."

"Naw, I kinda like the idea of bein' a soldier like Mr. Russell was tellin'."

Mirielle wrinkled her brow. "A soldier?"

"I like leadin'. Miss Calista says I'm a natural leader. If'n I could help people be free like yer doin' fer me and the guys, I could be a good captain or a general." He puffed out his chest and saluted.

"A captain or a general." She repeated, then tucked that away in her heart. Surely he was playing an imagination game like all boys do. He had to try on various professions through pretense. "Well, let's get you an excellent education so you have a choice on what you become, shall we?" The largest battle would be improving Frankie's command of English, not of men.

"Yes, ma'am." He grinned at her. "Ain't none of us that don't want three squares a day even if we have to get learned up to have 'em."

Learned up, you will be, young man. Mirielle held out a packet of addressed envelopes. "Would you see how many boys can deliver these?" Evan took half the invitation list to Calista first thing this morning. "Then Miss Calista may have another set that should be ready to go out as well."

"She said to tell you they'd be out by tomorrow." A quick whistle followed by three short ones brought all the newsies in earshot right to her, courtesy of Frankie's talent. A few minutes later, an organized delivery system worked out between them and the decorative personalized invitations, written in her finest calligraphy over many cups of coffee to keep her eyes open, took off to the wives of the most influential men in Helena. Falling asleep on a stack of envelopes almost derailed the project. Skipping breakfast caught up the lost time before classes started. The hunger reminded Mirielle exactly why the sacrifice of a little sleep and a missed meal made a difference. She'd felt them before—and the newsies dealt with hunger every day. Who knew if they felt safe enough to sleep through the night? No more! Not if she could change it.

She waved the boys off after instructing them to come to her classroom when finished. Frankie's gang wove through the downtown crowd before fanning out to make sure the ladies received their invitations. They'd wait and bring back the RSVP cards, if at all possible. Little worry bugs niggled their way into her thoughts like weevils in flour. What if no one came? Could she get more time if not enough people showed up? She mentally swatted the doubts away.

Mirielle pushed herself to remember someone much greater than she cared for the newsies. God had it all under control, whether her idea worked or not. She set her mind on the next phase. Each boy needed a portfolio for the potential sponsors. Calista, Albert, Evan, and all the boys would help create the portfolios as both introductions for the newsies and to highlight each boy's unique personality and talents. This time next week, the funding would be secure for all eleven boys.

Mirielle focused so intently on the vision of the

strategy to keep the boys safe in school, learning music, eating three meals a day, that the trolleys could crash right on top of her and she wouldn't know what happened. Until… she stopped short at bumping into someone.

"I apologize, Miss Sheehan." Mrs. Broadwater looked at her askance. "I'm sure I didn't mean to walk in your path. But those boys had me all turned around. Have you ever seen such a commotion?"

"No, I'm sorry. I was not watching where I was going. My fault, Mrs. Broadwater." Mirielle took a step to the side.

"Didn't I hear your name mentioned with a new gentleman caller?" She tapped a gloved finger against her chin. "Yes, I believe that's what I heard. Quite tall and handsome is how I heard it. Are we losing our new school teacher so quickly?"

"Ma'am?" Mirielle wrinkled her brow. "I haven't been—"

"Now don't pretend with me, young lady. I can see it written all over your face. Why you're perfectly moony-eyed."

"No, ma'am, I'm not—"

"Ladies," Evan tipped his top hat. "Miss Mirielle, I'm here to assist today. I hoped we'd hear some news as well."

"My, my. And you tried to pretend with me. Tsk, tsk." She waggled a finger. "You shouldn't be ashamed of step-ping out together. You make a lovely couple."

Flames shot into Mirielle's cheeks. "No! I mean, Mr. Russell and I aren't—"

"No?" Mrs. Broadwater's confusion halted her for only a moment. "Ah, I see. The two of you are as yet undeclared. Don't mind me. I won't tell a soul."

Mirielle tried again to clear the error, but despite her

ability to speak up for the boys, not one word could squeak through her tight throat defending herself.

Evan's eyes twinkled one second too long in Mirielle's mind before he answered. "Good afternoon, ma'am. I don't think we've been introduced." He held out a hand to greet the woman.

"Pardon my lack of manners, Mrs. Broadwater. This is Mr. Evan Russell, he's... uh... well he's..."

"Helping with the newsies reading lessons while they're helping me search for my son." His voice lowered. "You may have heard about the fire and the Russell family home last year."

"How tragic," she fluttered a hand in front of her mouth. "What a kind man you are, Mr. Russell, to give of yourself during your time of grief. I did hear of a new search for the little boy at my ladies' suffrage association this morning." Her eyes melted into motherly sympathy. "I so hope he's found."

"Thank you."

"How are the newsies able to help you, Mr. Russell?"

"We have an agreement. The boys are searching for any word of Joseph while I'm assisting Miss Mirielle in procuring educational sponsors for the newsies. I promised to be a sponsor for one myself."

"Sponsors?" If Mrs. Broadwater had been a cat, the hair on her scruff would be standing on end. "What would these sponsors do? No, the better question is, what can one do with those little hooligans?"

Mirielle rushed to the battle line with words she'd been rehearsing for the tea. Better she use them with this woman of influence or the tea might never happen. If she could turn this one negative woman around, the others were sure to follow. "Mrs. Broadwater, I'm pleased you recognize the need to help the newsies." She gave the brightest smile she could muster. "Maybe you could help us, too."

"Me?" She flattened her gloved hand across her heart. "You know one of those ruffians nearly gave me a heart attack landing on me in the trolley last week? I tell you, they have no discipline whatsoever." She shook her head and rolled her lips inward in distaste. "What in the world could I do for those uncouth youths?"

Mirielle pulled another idea from her recent read of Twain's book. This time she tried Huck Finn's charm. "I suppose I am asking too much. Perhaps another lady would better suit the situation." Before giving Mrs. Broadwater a chance to cut in again, she added while shaking her head in a slow, oh-so-sorrowful-a-manner. "It'd be too much of a bother to ask you to help entertain a society function. Don't I know how busy you are? Of course, I do. How could I even ask you to take the leadership role with the ladies of this city?" She paused for a moment and caught the twinkle in Evan's eyes.

As soon as Mrs. Broadwater opened her mouth, Mirielle continued to take away the opportunity she hadn't yet offered. "So inconsiderate of me for assuming you'd want to be the lady to lead the way. No, you're right, Mrs. Broadwater. Thank you." She moved a tad, as if to turn away. "It was good to see you —"

"You wait just a moment, Miss Sheehan. Just a moment now." Mrs. Broadwater laid fingertips on Mirielle's forearm.

"Yes, ma'am?" Mirielle blinked in innocence and glanced at Evan, as if confused.

A smile played around his mouth.

"If you need a society function led to get those boys off the street, then look no further. As the president of the ladies' auxiliary, it falls to me to provide opportunities to the cream of our society."

"You want to lead the tea to get sponsors for the newsies?"

"A simple tea? Why didn't you say so in the first place?"

"Well, I certainly don't want to impose on your good nature."

"What imposition? Anything to help get those children off the streets and into safe positions."

"Wonderful!" She clapped her gloves in muffled applause. "I'll just go let the newspaper know you will be our patron leading the charge." Mirielle leaned in toward Mrs. Broadwater. "You'll be touted as the woman who gave Helena its new model citizens. Goodness, you'll be considered a hero right up there with Lewis and Clark, who put Montana on the map."

Mrs. Broadwater giggled. "Well, dear, I don't think they'll go that far. Tell me what exactly we must raise."

"We only need ten more sponsors, so each boy will have full tuition, clothing, and school books until graduation. At graduation, our young men will have the education needed to find gainful employment right here in Helena."

"Here?" Mrs. Broadwater's face blanched. "In Helena? But I thought we were raising funds to send them away to training."

"Oh no, Mrs. Broadwater. Why send away such talented young men? They're so ambitious and studious. What would we do ten or fifteen years from now if some other town were so lucky as to get such driven, industrialists as those future leaders?"

"Well, I... I..." she stammered.

"We may not have gold and silver mines forever here in Helena, but we sure can mine the gold of our intelligent children for our future good." She took Mrs. Broadwater's elbow and walked with her toward the newspaper office. "Isn't it grand we see eye-to-eye? Those boys will be safely off the streets in no time with leaders like you at the helm."

Change a word or two and Mrs. Broadwater would be the patron matron over the project. The other women would drag their husbands to the tea just to rub shoulders with such a lady. Mirielle smiled at her. "Let's get your announcement into the paper right away. I see your patronage being so successful we might even be turning sponsors away."

"Then I suppose Mr. Broadwater and I ought to sponsor one of these future leaders before they're all gone?" Her voice squeaked at the end as she asked herself the question.

"What a good idea!" Mirielle nodded. "Can you imagine what it'll feel like to see a boy you sponsored grow up and graduate school? Won't you be proud that day!"

Mrs. Broadwater glowed. "Oh, won't that be a special occasion? Yes, I'm sure several of my friends will want to join in the effort." She tilted her head as if a thought grew into a tall tree. "Then what if my boy could lead other boys into a bright future?" The leaves on that tree burst forth. "Why, we could simply have built the next business generation!"

"So true, Mrs. Broadwater, so true." The lady had flipped from an antagonist to a passionate soldier of the mission to save the newsies. She needed only someone to plant the idea and then help her envision the fruit on that tree. Exactly the person at exactly the right time.

Mirielle sent a silent thank you to heaven. Then she tossed a glance over her shoulder, through Mrs. Broadwater's many-feathered hat, to see what had come of her new friend.

"I see another party in your future, Mrs. Broadwater. You may want to throw a huge graduation gala for all these boys. One the likes Helena has never seen before."

She almost laughed at Evan's bemused expression, but didn't want to spoil the possibilities buzzing around Mrs. Broadwater's head like bees swarming blossoms in the warm sunshine.

Evan picked up his pace, held the door, and followed the women inside the newspaper office.

Mirielle tucked his support inside her heart. There'd be time to examine it later. Right now, she'd turned a disgruntled lady into the second avid sponsor for her boys. Oh, that Mr. Twain knew how to handle people! But the bigger question remained—could eleven unruly boys really become future community leaders? Yes, and she intended to prove it one way or another.

CHAPTER 7

EVAN WALKED into the evening meeting for the Montana Club, the social group for millionaires. He still felt out of place, even though he'd been a member for several months. Membership was one door newfound mining wealth had opened for him. He enjoyed the opportunity to mingle with and learn from other community-minded men in business. Socially, these friends helped open more doors while he searched for his son. More than once, he'd been offered positions on boards in the community. So far, all understood the drive to find his missing boy. Though their expressions and support showed sympathy, it wasn't hard to tell his friends felt the search was coming to an expected, fruitless end. The meetings put him in contact with men that suggested visiting the posh private school in the first place. Until then, he could at least help the boys find sponsors.

Mr. Broadwater had the floor as Evan sidled along the wall of the overstuffed, smoke-filled room. "I say, five years has been long enough gathering at our offices."

"Indeed." Mr. Power answered, "I hear there's property available at Sixth and Fuller."

"Then why don't we form a committee and investigate. Our ranks are swelling." He waved a cigar in the air, gesturing around the room before settling an elbow on the table to point the butt at Evan. "There's standing room only as it is."

A chorus of male voices joined in agreement, "Here, here."

Mr. McDonald sat with the other businessmen around the enormous conference table in the Gold Block meeting rooms. He stood and scraped back a chair. "I better be getting on my way, gents. My wife hasn't stopped yammering at me to get home at an earlier hour since that last snow. She's still going on about the winter of '86 as if it happened yesterday." He shook hands with the men on either side of him as he worked his way out of the room. "Somehow I think that woman cares about this old hide of mine." A few chuckles acknowledged the admiration for the McDonald's long marriage record.

Evan felt the blood drain from his face. He froze as he had when he found Nadine, mostly covered by a drift. She'd curled into a ball at base of the barn door, beside the downed cow she'd tried to save. His small wife hadn't been able to push the door closed to keep the animal inside before the blizzard built up icy drifts against it. That winter stole his wife, ranch, and way of life. That winter caused such a deep desperation that he'd left Joseph with his brother's family, where the little boy should have been safe, instead of taking him into the dangers of mining camp life. That winter would only melt from memory when he knew Joseph was safe—or what happened to his little son.

Then Mr. McDonald noticed the effect his words caused. He stopped next to Evan. "Ah, son, I'm sorry. I wasn't thinking." He bowed his head as he lifted a hand on the younger man's shoulder. "You'll find him. Don't give up."

Evan blinked his eyes, coming back to the present. "Thank you. I won't." The quiet settled in the room as heavy as the dark night outside. Better to make it useful than leave all these men with a bitter taste. "Gentlemen, may I have the floor? There's been a development in the situation with the street boys you might want to be a part of..."

CHAPTER 8

COOKIES, coffee, hot cider for the children, and a bit of information about each newsie waited for the good-hearted people. Mirielle surveyed the room for any last minute forgotten detail. Each newsie had a small biographical page for the potential sponsors to consider. Instead of reading lessons, the boys had one-on-one assistance preparing small speeches for the coming attendees. Calista, Evan, and Albert helped her prep them. But one little boy failed to attend both times. Joey."Miss Mirielle?" Frankie peeked his head into the schoolroom.

She set down the last plate of cookies. "Frankie! Are all the boys with you?"

He moved into the doorway. "No, ma'am." His eyes shifted around the room rather than focusing on her.

"Is everything all right?" She scooted around the chairs set up for an audience in rows. "Is Joey sick? He hasn't been around all week. I'm worried."

"W-e-l-l..."

"Where is he? I'll go get him right now." She turned to pick up her coat.

"He's here."

"Here. Where here?" Leaving the garment untouched, Mirielle turned back to the boy. "Frankie, what's going on?" She leaned over him for a better view. Craning a glance around the corner into the hallway, a frightened Joey plastered himself against the wall as if hiding. Another questioning glance at Frankie's tight lips, and Mirielle crooked her finger and wiggled it, calling the younger boy into the room without a word.

Joey walked forward with halting steps.

"I'll ask one more time. You know you can trust me." She gave both boys direct eye contact. "What is going on?"

Joey crumbled into tears. "I don' wanna," he hiccupped. "I don' wanna leave Frankie."

"Honey," she knelt down and held her arms open. Joey melted into her embrace. "Honey, what makes you think you have to leave Frankie?" But the little guy just rolled his face back and forth on her shoulder.

"Miss Mirielle," Frankie stopped and took a deep breath. "Miss Mirielle," he started again, as if it took every ounce of courage he could muster. "I think I gotta be givin' Joey to Mr. Evan."

Mirielle gasped. She pried the tyke, who sobbed all the harder, away to look at his face. She squinted as she studied the dirty hair, shape of his eyebrows, and the rest of his face. "Why yes, you do have a resemblance under all that soot."

Joey pressed back into Mirielle's warm hug. "Don't let 'im take me."

"What's all the hubbub?" Evan asked as he walked into the classroom. "Did he bump a knee or noggin?"

Joey crumpled. The unexpected motion knocked Mirielle off her heels. Both child and teacher landed in a fluff of skirts on the floor.

Evan rushed to their aid as Frankie grabbed for Joey. Their heads knocked hard, landing them both right beside Mirielle and Joey. The surprise landings and stunned faces on all four caused Joey to crack a hint of a giggle. Just enough to release the tension and light laughter in Frankie and Evan as they both rubbed the tops of their heads at the same time.

"Let's stay put for a moment." Mirielle turned Joey around to sit in her lap and wrapped her arms around him. "I think we have a few minutes before anyone else arrives."

Frankie rolled his lips in and bobbed his head in the tiniest of motions.

"Anyone want to let me in on—" Evan's attention caught on Joey's face. He reached out to touch the boy's hair. But Joey jerked backward, away from Evan's hand. Evan dropped his hand into his lap. "Joseph?"

Even as he pressed backward against Mirielle, Joey asked, "Are you really my father?"

Before Evan could answer, Frankie put an arm around the younger boy. "I brought Joey 'cuz maybe you could be his daddy and he could be warm and safe. But jes soz you know, he don't wanna be here." Frankie's voice shook a little. "But I done told him if'n you was his daddy that he could grow up in a nice house with food every day 'stead of beggin' like we do." Frankie's chin lifted. His eyes shimmered while he worked to hold back the tears. His face contorted in pain as he tried swallowing the tears. "But before you take him," he gulped. "Before—" Frankie sniffed and focused on the corner of the room in silence as he visibly fought for self-control. He cleared his throat and tried again. "I jes wanna know he's really gonna be safe or you can't have him."

Frankie couldn't stop the hot tears banking over his efforts to hold them at bay. But he lifted his chin a tad bit higher, like a fox cub against a bear. He looked defeated, though he'd fight for his little brother to the end.

CHAPTER 9

TEARS COURSED down Evan's face. He let them flow, only wiping a few away so he could see his son. Joseph sat a hand's breath away. He wanted to hoot to the sky or dance in wild abandon, tossing his son high into the air and catching him again. But the boy looked ready to run at the slightest movement with a badger of a guardian watching out for him.

Evan chose his words and then delivered them quietly so the boys wouldn't spook at the powerful emotion raging inside his chest. "Frankie." He inclined his head with respect to the boy who'd protected an unrelated child like a brother. Then he turned to his son. "Joey, yes, I know you're my son. You have your mama's hair and the shape of her eyes. But see the color of mine? That's the color of yours."

Frankie leaned in to inspect Evan's eyes. And nodded.

"See the shape of your brow and nose?"

"No."

"Uh, sorry. Of course. We need a mirror."

Mirielle picked up Joey from her lap and set him near Frankie. "One moment. I have a compact in my reticule." She went to her desk, retrieved it, and knelt beside the boys. "Take a look. I think you'll see what we all can see."

Joey stared hard into the mirror. Then up at Evan, whose tears had dried but his face shone with joy.

Looking back into his reflection, Joey's finger traced an eyebrow. He looked back and Evan and held up the same finger toward his father's face.

Evan leaned into Joey's hand and the little boy traced his father's eyebrows, nose, and chin.

"What do you think?" Mirielle asked. "Would you like to get to know your daddy?"

A small whisper from Joey made them all lean in to hear. "Yes, but I don't wanna leave Frankie."

Evan accepted his comment, thought for a moment, and then smiled. "Frankie, he says you made him come. You had all the last week and a few days. But why did you bring Joey today and not another day?"

"I wasn't sure before."

"You weren't sure of what?"

"I found Joey. He was kind of a mess of a little kid. But —" he shrugged as he wiped his nose on a sleeve.

Both Mirielle and Evan waited and allowed Frankie to tell his story.

"It was hard to be alone, and he didn't eat much. But it's been hard to get him shoes and a coat and stuff. When you showed up lookin' fer him, at first I thought you'd jes be takin' him away." He looked at Joey. "Then I remembered what the pastor said about puttin' others first. I wanted to make sure Joey had a chance even if I didn't." He lowered his eyes.

"When you gave me your word, did you mean it?" Evan asked.

"Yeah. I gave my word." Another tear threatened Frankie's composure. "But I had to be sure you was who you said you was, and he was the son you lost."

"Even if it means you'll lose Joey, you still want to make sure he's safe back with me?"

"Yeah," Frankie's voice dropped to a low whisper. "It's the right thing to do."

"Frankie, I can't tell you how much I appreciate the care and love you've given Joseph." Evan cocked his head to the side, trying to catch Frankie's line of sight. "You remember I also gave my word on something, don't you?"

He nodded. "Yeah, I'm glad one of the boys is gonna get you as a sponsor, sir."

Evan shook his head. "Not just one of the boys, Frankie, I'd be honored if it would be you."

"Me?" Frankie's head popped up. Then he wrinkled his brow. "I can't accept."

"Why in the world not?" Mirielle asked, her brows furrowed. "Frankie, you can't pass up this opportunity."

He shook his head with a sad expression, but he squared his shoulders as if resolved. "I got more guys out there, Miss Mirielle. I can't leave 'em all. I can't leave one of 'em. They gotta have a leader. Someone to help 'em learn how to survive."

Evan answered, "I'll tell you what, Frankie—"

"Son, I say you give the rest of us a chance." Mr. Broadwater called into the room, startling all four of them. Mrs. Broadwater stood next to him with a hankie pressed to her cheek. Behind them, quite a crowd gathered, waiting in the hall respectfully.

The boys jumped up quick as hotcakes flipping on a griddle.

Mirielle sighed as Evan offered his hand to help her to her feet. She draped elegant fingers across his palm. With radiating excitement, she stood and then leaned in to him. "I think it's all going to work out, Mr. Russell. We're going to build a life for these boys!"

He pulled her fingers to his lips and kissed them. He looked into the depths of her soul and said, "Yes. We are."

"Isn't that so romantic?" Mrs. Broadwater asked a little too loudly of Mrs. McDonald. Other invited guests continued to fill the room and join in the social festivities. "And they say they aren't courting. Pooh."

Mirielle pinked all the way into her brunette tresses. "Mrs. Broadwater—"

Evan interrupted. "Yes, Mrs. Broadwater, I'm declaring my intentions to court Miss Sheehan," he looked only at her, willing a positive response, "if she'll accept."

Mirielle's pretty mouth opened a tiny bit before she clamped it shut. Would she agree? The seconds ticked away in silence.

"I, uh," she dipped her head and peeked up through her lashes. "I would like that, Mr. Russell."

The two ladies and a few of their friends clapped in glee.

"Now that's settled as I knew it would be." Mrs. Broadwater slipped an arm around Mirielle's waist. "Shall we choose our proteges?"

Evan looked down at the two boys near him and shrugged. They shrugged back with grins on their faces.

Frankie spoke first, "Womenfolk. They sure go fer that sweet stuff."

Evan broke out in laughter. "Makes life awfully nice for the menfolk though."

Frankie sagely nodded. "I like their cookies."

Evan ruffled the boy's hair. "I have a surprise for everyone, including Miss Mirielle. Would you get the other boys and help me?"

Frankie called his team to follow. A few minutes later, they reemerged with huge grins. Each boy carried either a drum, a penny whistle, or a hand drum. Except one youngster carried bagpipes.

The crowd burst into applause.

Mirielle wove through the crowd. "How in the world did you do this?"

He gestured around the room to the other men, tipping a nod to him here and there. "I had a little help from the Montana Club members."

"It's just wonderful!" She turned back with a worried look. "But I don't play or teach bagpipes."

"Ah, but Mr. McDonald does." He shook hands with the older man. "Miss Mirielle Sheehan, I'd like to introduce you to Mr. McDonald. He and his wife would like to sponsor the boy with the bagpipes. That lucky young man will get instruction on the instrument and, should he earn his grades as expected, on graduation will also be granted an internship at Mr. McDonald's import business. He has a series of warehouses and needs to raise up management to take over for him."

"How did you figure all that out?" Mirielle asked.

He felt like a hero in her eyes. "It wasn't hard. We had a talk the other day at the club meeting. A few of the members took it upon themselves to get the donated instruments."

"But the McDonald's?"

"They have no children to inherit. Jonathan is one of the older newsies. If he can prove himself a talented student, he'll get quite the opportunity starting in management with Mr. McDonald's business dealings."

One-by-one, they sponsored the boys by the end of the tea. Those sponsors would also act as mentors with regular visits to help the boys continually learn social skills. Their speeches drew both adoration and chuckles from the crowd. Two hours went by faster than his hat had the day he dropped it into the stream accidentally. It was out of sight before he'd taken three steps.

"That's it, Frankie. I bet you fellas are tuckered out." Evan put an arm around the lad and gave him a quick squeeze.

"Yup. Speechifying's real hard."

Evan laughed. "Yes, it is. Looks like the speechifying worked. Every boy has their sponsor—except one." Evan held out a hand. "Shake on it?"

Frankie's eyes lit up. "Yes, sir." As they shook, Frankie tossed out a question. "You gonna take Joey now you kept yer word?" He tucked both hands in his pockets and waited.

Evan put his hands in his pockets, too. "I haven't had a chance to think it all through yet, have you?"

Frankie didn't speak. He just looked at his shoes and wagged his head back and forth a little.

"What would you think if I rented a room next to mine for the two of you?"

"Can't do it, Mr. Evan. Got my guys to think about, you know." He tossed a side-glance at his new sponsor before resuming his downward gaze. "I think Joey's gonna need some time. He used ta have some real bad nightmares after I found him. Sometimes they come back."

Evan twisted his bottom lip to the side, scrunching up his lips as he considered the problem. He kept the fact his gut wrenched at Frankie's revelation to himself. "That's a hard one."

"Yeah. But we been doin' good before you came." He rocked back and forth, heel to toe and back again as if he rolled on a log.

"Surviving is good." He offered a cautious response. If Frankie changed his mind and bolted with Joey, it'd be a hard road finding them again. "You never know when things might go south."

The boy-man took another soul-wrenching look into Evan's eyes. "What d'ya say we let Joey get ta knowin' ya first?" Frankie patted Joey's shoulder. "He'll come around."

"What do you say I make sure all you boys get back to the Shanahan's each night for the time being? I hear they make sure you're all safe in the carriage house and their footman stays too."

Frankie gave a slight smile with grudging admiration in his eyes. "You been doin' some checkin' on us." Then he turned to face Evan and stuck out his hand. "Man-to-man, I give you my word. I'll help Joey get ready to come be with you."

He repeated their earlier test. "You good for your word?"

Stretching to his tallest, Frankie said, "Yep. You good fer yers?"

"You better believe I am." Evan accepted the boy's handshake without scoffing at a boy playing a grown up role. So much maturity, not yet a man but trying hard to act like one. It was his turn to admire Frankie. "If you'll help finish the cleanup and bring the newsies together, I'll let Miss Mirielle know our plan so she won't worry." *Though I will, until Joseph is safe with me.* But forcing the matter when the boys had shown themselves both trustworthy wouldn't rebuild a strong relationship with his son or his new ward.

CHAPTER 10

IT WAS the hardest moment of his life when Evan let his
son leave the safety of the wagon, even on such a mild
night. Holding himself back, watching Joseph walk away
after just finding him, ripped Evan's heart raw. That
Mirielle insisted on coming helped. He knew she'd hold
him accountable if he backed down. But more than that, he
drew strength from her presence.

"I know it's going against every ounce of your parent-
ing." Mirielle slipped her hand into his. "But winning Joey
over isn't about this one night."

"I know." Evan's voice rattled roughly in his throat as he
tore his gaze from the closed door. This one night meant
taking a risk that felt deeper and wider than the Missouri
River during a flash flood. What if something happened?
What if they ran?

The Shanahan's footman, Warren, came from the back
of the big house with a lantern. "They're all back safe and
tucking in for the night?"

"Yes," Evan's heart tightened.

"Miss Calista mentioned little Joey turned out to be your lost son. Congratulations!"

When had he last tucked Joseph in and told him a bedtime story? Would he be too old for that now? How much more time would pass before they'd be reunited for good? But out loud, he said, "Thank you for your constant care."

"It's nothing, sir. My rooms are out here and I'm enjoying the company." He waited politely. "Sir, is there anything more?"

Mirielle touched his shoulder. "We should go on now. Warren won't let any harm come to them."

Evan stared at the red brick carriage house. "Let me know if the boys need anything, won't you?"

"I will. And sir, it'll be my pleasure to keep my eye on your boy for you. Don't be concerned."

Evan gave a nod. He envisioned a completely different reunion. A little boy excitedly hugging him, jumping up and down, and wanting to be with his father. Not a frightened child, with no solid memory of who his father was, clinging to a stranger. The few words were all he could muster. "Well, thank you and goodnight then."

With a heart screaming inside, Evan helped Mirielle up into the bench seat. Then climbed up next to her and adjusted the lap robes. All the while, Evan chastised himself for leaving. What more could he do? He flicked the reins.

Mirielle didn't try to talk him out of his head, ply him with platitudes or verses. She simply asked questions to help him think rationally until a few blocks later, Evan pulled the horses to a halt and hung his head. "I can't do this, Mirielle. Not after all the searching."

She placed a hand over his wrist. "If you go back and grab Joey, what then?"

"Neither decision feels right or safe or smart." He couldn't go forward. He couldn't go back.

"Taking Joey out of the situation he'd grown used to, and where he felt safe, won't solve anything." She squeezed his wrist gently. "He doesn't know you, but I think he wants to."

Everything hinged on building a relationship with a son who didn't know him and who he didn't know. He had to trust God—and two scared boys—or lose Joseph all over again because of pushing too hard.

"Evan." She lifted her hand to his cheek, applying a light pressure.

He caught her gloved hand against his face like a lifeline and leaned into her palm. As if Mirielle's lips held the elixir of hope, Evan leaned in and sipped of that hope, never releasing her compassionate touch, warm against his skin through a layer of fine, thin wool.

EVAN'S GENTLE KISS LIFTED, HIS LIPS HOVERED slightly above hers. Mirielle didn't move a hair as his forehead rested against hers. She'd known this man less than two weeks, yet she knew with every bit of her body that she belonged here. With him. This man needed her and loved her. She knew it without a word spoken. His actions, attitude, and ability to be unabashedly vulnerable told her so much more than the pretty words she thought would be so important when she gave her heart away. Right now, Evan needed unconditional love to give him the strength to be patient with his son. Right now, Evan needed her words to get through the night alone.

He gently released Mirielle. "I don't know what to do about my son." He offered a tentative smile. "But I think we have something growing between us and I'm grateful you're not slapping me."

She laughed lightly at his unexpected humor. "No, I'm not interested in slapping you." She touched her bottom lip. "I… I… the kiss was lovely." Mirielle lowered her lashes, took a breath, and looked back up. "If you wouldn't mind driving me the rest of the way home, I wouldn't mind if you, uh, kissed me goodnight." She felt the heat in her cheeks as she spoke. Mirielle glanced at him from under her lashes again. "I think we have growing a relationship, too. You'll probably need less time for growing a relation-ship with Joey, but if it takes a little longer, promise me you'll be patient. In his heart, he knows where he belongs."

He looked behind, from the way they'd come, and then to the road ahead. "I will do my best. But leaving him. I never wanted to do that again." He sighed. "You have to understand that."

"What if you talked with Albert and Calista about staying in the carriage house with the boys until he's ready? You could be close to Joey while you two get to know one another again. Then you could keep an eye out for all the boys until you find more permanent living arrangements than the hotel. It can't be easy for Warren to do by himself."

Evan's eyes lit up. "Brilliant!" He planted a fast kiss smack on her lips this time. "You don't suppose I could—"

"No." She lifted an eyebrow as only a school marm could.

He took one glance at her face in the moonlight and capitulated. "Right. I'll put that plan into action first thing in the morning." Evan lifted the reins. The horses picked up on his fresh energy and pranced in place, ready to respond on command. "Thank you."

"For what?"

"For helping me do what's right for my son tonight. For helping me to find him in the first place. I just wish I could have scooped up all those boys and given them a home."

Mirielle nodded and tucked her hand through his bent elbow. "Yes, I wish I could do that too. Maybe a way will present itself. I'll be praying on that idea."

Evan looked at her for a long moment, then finally said, "Yes, I'll be praying on that, too."

CHAPTER 11

TWO WEEKS LATER, the newsies all sat in a semi-circle for their first music lesson. Mirielle's heart tripped at the sight. It'd taken a committee from the school board and the new educational sponsors, but they'd hammered out a schedule of classes. The plan included meal and manners training that the other children received from home. Since the dormitory was already filled with students during the first school semester, the newsies continued to live in the Shanahan's carriage house. But Evan carted them back and forth to school each day, sharing duties with Warren, in his large wagon refitted to seat the boys instead of hauling mining equipment. "Boys, I realize you are just beginning to read words. You know that's how we build sentences that create the stories you love." She lifted her conductor's baton to show them. "Now we're going to learn to read music to create songs."

Wide-eyed stares met her like she'd stumbled into a thicket full of deer. All eleven boys looked ready to take flight as she watched them look toward the exit as one unit. The humorous sight made it hard to hold back a chuckle. But for the sake of her new students' pride, she did. "It will not be as hard as you think. In fact, you all just did something together, at the same time. That's called acting in unison. And that's where we start." She tapped a few beats on the music stand in front of her. "That's a rhythm. Now you try in unison."

Mirielle chose to teach first using the drums. The boys that had drums shared a stick with the boy next to them. They practiced tapping the tips as she counted measures. By the end of their first class, the newsies all understood what whole, half, quarter, and eighth notes meant.

"You're all going to be wonderful! Instruments get put away properly and you're free to go out to the yard." She applauded their first-timer results.

Evan joined in clapping from where he'd leaned against the doorjamb, observing. "Here, here!"

Bright eyes and excited faces shone around the room. Chatter started about building snowmen, a game of tag, or a game of stickball.

"Miss Mirielle, may I have a word with you?" Evan proffered a brown paper bag toward the boys. "And for all you musical men, I've brought a reward. I hope you like peppermint sticks."

A second or less and Evan nearly went under the mob of children running to him for a candy. A moment later, all the boys had exited engaged in the various stages of donning new coats, scarves, and boots. They were out the door in seconds, leaving the youngest, Joey, hopping after, on one foot, calling for the others to wait.

Evan caught up to him and knelt to help. "How about we work together so you can get out there faster?"

Joey balanced on his father's shoulder, sticking his foot into the big hands waiting to assist. "Thanks, Pa." He grinned, showing a newly missing tooth.

"You're welcome, Joey." Evan grinned back and tweaked his nose. Pointing at a haphazardly worn boot, he said, "Stomp on it to make sure it's on all the way."

Joey obediently stomped. Then he threw his arms around Evan's neck in a big hug. "I'm glad you're back."

Mirielle's heart tripped a second time at Evan's stunned expression. She laid a hand over her heart, but stayed as silent as possible to avoid spoiling the moment.

"Oh, Joey, there's nowhere else I'd ever want to be but with you." His arms folded around the boy's small back and his eyes closed until Joey pushed away.

"Gotta go or I'll be last up to bat." He turned back at the open door. "See ya after school, Pa."

"See ya. I'll be right here waiting."

Joey smiled that one-tooth-missing grin. "I know." And he was out the door in a flash, slamming it behind him.

Mirielle let loose a giggle. "Evidently, telling them they don't live in a barn isn't quite going to work for slamming doors, is it?"

Evan laughed with her and shook his head. "Not today." He walked into the classroom. "But what if it were true, say, in a few weeks?"

"What do you mean?" Mirielle jumped up and threw her arms around his neck. "Oh! You found a place for the newsies!" She hugged him tight in celebration.

"Yes, and more if you think it might work." Evan pulled back and looked down into her eyes.

She wrinkled her nose at him. "Of course it'll work out. They'll follow you anywhere now."

He captured her hands and held them to his heart. "Mirielle." He took a deep breath. "I'm not talking about whether the newsies will follow me. I'm asking if you will."

"Are you—"

"Mirielle, will you marry me?"

To her, Evan appeared a tad worried. He'd had enough of that as far as she was concerned. She didn't want to cause him another moment of worry in his entire life. Mirielle smoothed his brow and brushed the hair from his forehead. "I will follow you anywhere, too."

"Even into a household full of eleven rowdy boys?"

She smiled into his eyes. "Even there." Then she forced a frown. "But what if I want more boys?"

"You think we need more boys?"

"Maybe one or two we create together? Or girls." She nodded. "Yes, maybe we need a girl."

He laughed. "I wouldn't know what to do with one among all those—" a snowball hit the wall of the building followed by a series of several more. "She better be able to throw a mean snowball."

In the most serious manner possible, Mirielle nodded. "She'll have eleven brothers to defend her if she can't."

"So that's a yes?"

"Are you good for your word?" Mirielle stuck out her hand, unable to stop the mirth from showing on her face.

"I am." He took her hand in his. "Are you?"

"I am." As she shook on it, Evan tugged her into his arms. She let out a gleeful squeal, ending in a spurt of laughter against his chest.

He wrapped his arms around her and sealed the deal with a kiss.

EPILOGUE

IT WAS the slowest bridal march ever played. But the Newsies Pipe and Drum Corps squawked it out to the best of their ability. Mendelssohn's Wedding March was also the only song they'd had time to learn, lasting all of eight measures. They repeated those same eight measures over and over until Mirielle made it to the front of the church.

Evan whispered into her ear. "Seemed you went a little fast. Are you excited to start our life together?"

She squeezed his hand and whispered back. "Shh, yes. But I didn't want to torture the guests any more than I had to." She took a peek over his shoulder. "Look. Just about everyone is plugging their ears."

His shoulders shook with laughter, but he kept it from being heard. "This time next year and they'll be in demand for their talents."

The priest cleared his throat and leaned in to join the whispering couple. "Maybe the year after that." The glint in his eye nearly caused both Mirielle and Evan to laugh out loud. "Shall we begin?"

SAMPLE: HEART OF THE ROCKIES...

This lovely story shares the early days of women in swimming nearing the turn-of-the-century when traditional sensibilities conflict with modern ideas. How does a traditional man learn to love a woman with modern ideas?

Could she believe in herself when no one else did?

1892, Helena MT: Delphina O'Connor believed God-given dreams for women didn't stop at marriage and children. Hers might not include a husband or family at all. So, when Hugh Thomas rescues the new swimming instructor at the elegant Broadwater Natatorium from near drowning in the Victorian-styled resort pool, how can anyone believe the freedom to enjoy swimming, competition, and a healthy body is an appropriate activity for a proper lady? Hugh is about to find out status quo is the starting line for a courageous woman with a dream!

Explore the elaborate genuine history of the Broadwater Hotel and Natatorium through romantic fiction, though you'll meet several iconic people from Montana's authentic history in these pages. You might even meet your own ancestor as Angela Breidenbach weaves genealogical and historical tidbits like Easter eggs into this fun glimpse of Montana's elegant past. Once the richest city in the world with millionaires galore, this Gilded Age society exists only in our memory. But what a memory she left us!

Heart of the Rockies explores the real-world question: What do you do when you think differently than the world around you?

HEART OF THE ROCKIES, BOOK 3

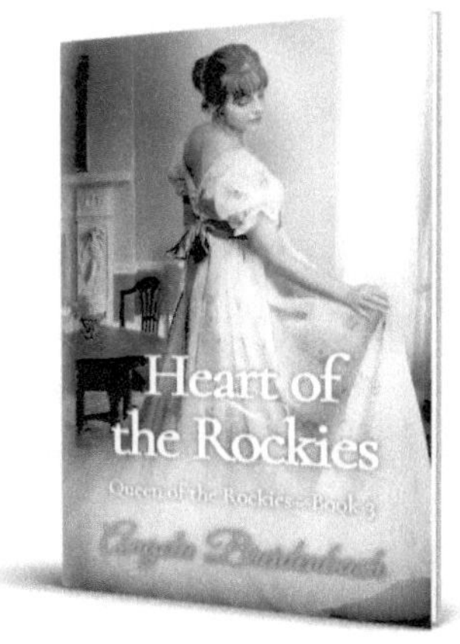

∼

Late winter, 1892, Helena, MT

Delphina O'Connor ran to the edge of the plunge. "Kick up!" Was that Mr. Broadwater's daughter in the deep end? Delphina strained to see in the darker waters of the deep end. The electric lamplight didn't quite reach far enough to tell who fell in, but she wasn't succeeding in getting out!

The young girl thrashed against the heavy woolen skirt of her swim costume. She couldn't keep her head above the hot springs pumped into the monstrous indoor pool.

Grabbing the pole hook from the wall, Delphina stretched out as far as she could. But soon the youngster would no longer break the surface to see the lifesaver. "Calm down, grab on!"

Panicking, she took in more water than air. Terror overtook the waterlogged child as she thrashed and knocked the pole away. Delphina couldn't get hold of the swim outfit either. It slipped off the hook each time the girl twisted. The girl's hands couldn't reach the surface in the twelve-foot depths, and she was fatiguing fast.

Bubbles.

Knowing how to swim wouldn't help when both woolen skirts would drag them down. But she had to try. "Help! I need help!" A quick glance around proved no one else had entered the natatorium yet. Did no one hear her scream?

She threw the pole hook on the deck, took a deep

breath, and jumped. Warm water sucked her under as she swam hard. She kept her eyes on the dark, descending figure as the girl went limp. Kicking her swimming slippers as hard as she could, Delphina managed to get a hand on the girl's billowing sleeve and yanked at the material. But she couldn't budge the weight of sopping wool more than a smidgeon. The girl was closer to Delphina's size than she'd realized. Both costumes swirled around them like the jelly-fish in an inky dark ocean.

She pointed her shoulders at the plunge wall and kicked harder, with every ounce of effort in her being, until her legs burned and her arms felt numb. For a moment, the surface tickled at her face, but Delphina couldn't stretch above it to catch the air she needed to propel them both to safety and gulped half water with the oxygen. Delphina willed her body, and the one she towed upward. Instead of surfacing for air, the two sank further toward the bottom. The skylights retreating into pinpoints of blurred light. Burning lungs, a screaming cough clawing at her throat, Delphina refused to let go of the adolescent.

Muscular arms closed around her torso from behind and thrust her toward the surface. Still, she wouldn't release the ruffle her fingers clutched. Up. Up. More arms grabbed at hers and fought to pry the limp girl away as liquid gave way to air.

Delphina sucked in half a stomach full of water as she gasped for life a moment too soon. Then she choked, coughed, and heaved out what she'd taken in. Nose burn-ing, ragged gasps, and more coughing racked her ribs until she fell exhausted on the pool deck, trembling from the exertion. A shadow fell on her face, blocking the natural light from the natatorium's windows high above.

A man's voice directed towards the skirmish further down the planked deck. "Arms above her head. Press her stomach." He called orders to others even as the man's big hands thrust Delphina's arms above her head. "Turn her over and get the water out of her." He flipped Delphina like a rag doll and spanned her back with one hand. He waited for a breath, then flapjacked her back and watched her face for signs of life. Seeming satisfied, he stood and turned to supervise the boys following his lifesaving orders.

The shadow man moved away, leaving Delphina sprawling on the pool deck in the least ladylike manner, skirts as scattered as driftwood. Lifting to her elbows, Delphina watched Wilder spew more water than a body should be able to hold. But she survived! Delphina lay back and thanked God. She took a deep breath, grateful for the other rescuers and the sweet feeling of dry air moving in and out of her chest.

Her rescuer returned. "What do you think you two were doing swimming in the deep end in those costumes?"

She'd feel much more comfortable if the man's features were visible. After all, he'd had his hands all over her. But the light pouring in from the windows above produced backlighting, drowning his face in shadows. "What?" Delphina's head throbbed, and her ears needed unclogging.

He fired off another question like dynamite near the mines. "Don't you know better?"

She squeezed her burning eyes and blinked a few times, trying to distinguish more about the man towering above than the outline of his legs askew, fists jammed on hips. His darker hair dripped down on her like rain spattering saturated ground. As her vision adjusted to the ethereal illusions of color in geometric patterns created by the immense stain glass windows, electric lamps, and arced cathedral ceilings inside the natatorium, his angry eyes crackled like lightning over the Montana mountains.

"What?" She shook her head and blinked hard as she threw the heavy braid behind her shoulder. The length and weight of the sopping plait so great it slapped the wooden floor like a mop.

"I said," he paused, creating a stern effect, "you obviously need to return to your governesses. The two of you almost drowned."

Governesses? "I don't need a governess. I am—"

"If you can't avoid danger by yourself, then you must be under the care of an adult."

Enough. Only her first day in position and already a near drowning incident. Delphina shoved to her shaking knees and then to standing. The heavy skirts of the swimming costume threatened to drag her right back down. Planting her hands on her hips as he'd done, she snapped back, "I am an adult, sir, and I'll have you know—"

"Adults don't behave irresponsibly." He glared at her.

She wanted to scream at this insulting stranger. Then she remembered he'd saved not only her life, but also Wilder's. The girl who was in her care and the daughter of her new employer. She closed her eyes and deliberately lowered her hands to her sides with a long, long inhale and exhale. "First, let me say thank you."

"Don't. Just be more careful." He called to the dozen or so gathered around them. "Boys, let's get all this gear cleaned up and ready for laps."

She tightened her lips against her teeth. Teeth that wanted to bite all of a sudden at his imperial tone. "Sir, I was not irresponsible. I was, in fact, trying to save Miss Broadwater."

His head jerked back in surprise. For a moment, his handsome face registered astonishment… and then he chuckled. The chuckle rippled into an all-out laugh thundering as it echoed in the cavernous building.

Delphina's face rushed with warmth. "That's quite enough, sir. You may have saved our lives." She looked around at the other dripping young men gathered around them. "But you have no right to insult either one of us. Exactly who are you anyway?"

"Hugh Thomas, the swimming instructor, luckily for you. And you would be?"

Her eyes narrowed. "Ah, the swimming instructor for the men." What a chauvinist! "I would be the scientific and ornamental swimming instructress for the women."

The man's eyebrows lifted. "The what?" He jolted with a laugh and then sobered when he took a look at the group helping Wilder Broadwater. He shook his head, flinging water droplets around them. "Then I'll suggest you be replaced immediately."

She gasped. Unfortunately, as she did, the water still streaming from her hair sucked into her windpipe. Coughing the water out of her lungs doubled Delphina over and delayed the dramatic delivery she'd planned.

She pointed a finger at him until she rose to standing. To her surprise, he waited. "You'll do no such thing!" Her words would be so much more convincing if she didn't cough through the water streaming down her face from the mass of tangled hair.

"Just get it all out." He landed several smart slaps on

her back, causing more hacking than necessary, in Delphina's opinion. "You'll feel much better."

"You—" She held up a hand, signaling for him to stop and jammed the other against the unexpected sharp stitch in her side. "Don't touch me!" Her words came out more like a hoarse tom cat.

He walked away. "Miss Broadwater, let's get you to a chair." As he gently sat the teary girl on a chair, one of the many young men grabbed and deposited nearby. "Towels? Let's get some towels around these girls."

Delphina's eyes widened. He could be kind to Antoinette Wilder Broadwater, but not to the woman who tried to save her life? What an impolite heathen! Then the warmth of a towel wrapped around Delphina, and a gangly boy propelled her to another chair near Wilder's.

She looked up and nodded her appreciation. "Thank you."

He answered with a kind voice, "My pleasure, miss."

Hugh's directions scrambled the group into action as they cleaned the deck of lifesaving equipment. "Frankie, throw on a dry robe and fetch Miss Broadwater's parents. They'll want to know immediately."

"Yes, sir, Mr. Thomas." The boy that'd been caring for Delphina bobbed his head and took off to his errand.

What was he, all of fourteen? Still, he had more manners than his uncouth instructor. But Wilder had been given into her care this afternoon. "I'll get your mother, Wilder." Delphina rose, but the low chair caught at her swimming costume. She fell forward, catching herself on the heels of her hands, preventing her face from smacking into the wood deck, but splayed on the ground in a most unladylike fashion—again.

"Miss O'Connor!" Wilder called. "Are you all right?"

The next second, strong hands clasped around her waist and hauled her up to her feet like a pile of laundry. "Go on, Frankie. I have this under control."

Delphina closed her eyes to stop the tears of both pain and embarrassment, as she pressed hot, stinging hands against the cooler folds of the wet swim skirt. "Thank you," she swallowed her pride. "Thank you, again." Delphina could not bring herself to offer even a polite smile.

He stood too close, hands still on her waist, and leaned down to her ear so only she could hear him. "I fear dance instructor is not a good idea either." His chuckle tickled the skin behind her ear.

Why did his voice sing in her veins?

THE GIRL'S EYES SPARKED A DEEP AMBER FIRE. She shook free of his sturdy hands. "Unbelievable!" She pushed him away. "You have no idea who I am or what I'm capable of and yet you presume to judge my abilities!"

He wanted to laugh at the girl smoothing the mass of sopping hair out of her eyes, but the seriousness of lives nearly lost subdued Hugh. "What I know is you're too young and inexperienced for this position."

Wilder chose this moment to pipe up. "Oh, Miss O'Connor's not too young. She's a spinster."

At the child's unfiltered input, the swim instructress nearly turned purple under the tangled mass of hair the color of evergreen bark after a downpour on a spring day.

Hugh couldn't help himself. He tossed off a grin that broke into a rumbling laugh. "I see."

"Wilder!" Miss O'Connor spun to chastise the owner's daughter. Then she obviously grappled for words before giving up and turning back on him. "I'll have you know, sir, that I have a teaching degree from Vassar and that I focused on the science of health—and that includes an excellent knowledge of swimming and lifesaving."

"Then you of all people should know better than to swim with all," he gestured at the voluminous swimwear, "that on in the deep end of a pool."

"I did not—"

"Wilder, oh Wilder," Mrs. Broadwater swept into the natatorium. "Dear heart, please tell me you're all right." She clasped the wet girl tightly to her bosom, not caring about her clothing.

"I believe she'll be fine, ma'am."

"Is that the case, Miss O'Connor?"

"I'm sorry, Mrs. Broadwater, I haven't been able to check Wilder myself. I've been," she tipped her head toward Hugh, "detained for questioning."

"Wilder, what happened?" Mrs. Broadwater pulled her daughter's chin up with her hand and scrutinized her.

"Mama, I ran out to place a candy order for after swimming. You know how hungry I get after being in the water." She hung her head. "But I slipped in when I went around that corner." She pointed to where the railing stopped. Her shoulders slumped as her mother's eyes narrowed. "Miss O'Connor jumped in after me. Then all these boys saved us both."

"Candy." Hugh choked back a growl. "You both almost drowned for a candy?"

Wilder's eyes brimmed. "I didn't mean to do that." Puppy dog eyes plead up at her parents as Mr. Broadwater joined the crowd.

"Ah, but you did, young lady." Her father's stern voice caused a cavalcade of tears. He peered through round spectacles at his pocket watch. "The counter isn't open for another thirty minutes. What possessed you to race in so early?"

She mumbled, "I didn't think Mama would let me have any." Tears streaked down her cheeks.

Miss O'Connor popped into the momentary lull. "Wilder, this is exactly why the rules for not running on the deck are there. With your parents as the owners, it's even more important for you to set the example for the other girls and boys who come to take a plunge." Then she turned to the Broadwaters. "Would you consider sitting your daughter out for the next class as a discipline? She should have to dress out and sit on the side so she can still learn from the instruction."

Evidently, Miss O'Connor told the truth. But was she their governess or his employee?

"No, Papa! That's not fair!"

"I think that's not fair either, my girl." He agreed.

"But sir—" Miss O'Connor started.

He held up a hand. "I didn't build this entire resort just to have my only daughter misuse it. Nor did I build this natatorium to lose her." Charles Broadwater pursed his lips as everyone waited for his decision. "Wilder will sit out, as you've suggested. In addition, the temptation that caused the poor behavior is also removed." He directed his attention to the young girl. "You've also lost your purchasing privileges at the shop yonder for the classes Miss O'Connor chooses to sit you out."

"Papa, that's really not fair!" She whined.

"I will notify the staff. Should Miss O'Connor need to make this decision again, the two parts will make the whole."

"But—"

"Evidently I need to add more discipline before you learn a lesson?"

She hung her head, light hair and a limp blue ribbon drooped over her shoulders in a stringy mass. Poor girl resembled more of a cocker spaniel at the moment. "No, sir."

Hugh folded his arms. He rather liked his employer's way of thinking and handling of his daughter. The colonel hadn't once raised his voice. "Sir, if I may, the women cannot survive in the deep end. Twelve feet is not safe for a lady, even one who thinks she can swim." Then he pointedly glanced in Miss O'Connor's direction. "Might I suggest a cord across the pool at the four-foot mark? I don't believe the ladies should venture deeper than four feet. The risk, as we've seen, is too great."

"Just one minute. There's no need to limit the ladies to the shallow end." Miss O'Connor leapt to the defense of womankind everywhere. "This was an unusual circumstance. In fact, I've been able to swim—"

"I did not see proof of that today, Miss O'Connor." He stepped closer. "In fact, I saw exactly the opposite as I saved your life."

Everyone craned to catch up with the last banter, bebopping back and forth between them like birdies on the badminton court. "Indeed, you did not, sir!" As her hair dried, it unraveled into frizzy ropes that hung like Rapunzel's locks. Did she know how comical she appeared? "What you saw were two bodies fighting heavy woolens in the water. You did not see my lack of ability to swim. You couldn't have—"

"You're making the point, Miss O'Connor. I pulled you both up with great effort and then all these boys assisted getting you and Wilder on the deck."

"Why was that, Mr. Swim Instructor? Were we too heavy for you to get out of the water yourself?"

Mr. Swim Instructor.

"I do believe you've made my point."

He meant to answer. He opened his mouth, about to, and then Hugh realized she was right. All five foot two of her and he'd needed help with the weight of those skirts.

Colonel Broadwater took the reins of the conversation. "What I'm hearing is that my daughter nearly drowned because of her swim costume and that her teacher, and a very fit man, both had trouble because of these contraptions you ladies wear. Is that what you're telling me?"

Both instructors answered at once, "Yes." Their eyes were drawn to one another. Hugh's were then drawn down the drenched lady in front of him. He couldn't really tell much of any detail under all that droopy black fabric. How many sheep were shorn for that outfit? Was there a woman under there? But something about the flaring fire in her eyes made him swallow. Hard.

"Besides my daughter's safety, these swimming costumes are putting any lady that enjoys the natatorium at risk. Is that what you're telling me?"

Miss O'Connor nodded vigorously at his words while Hugh contemplated the unknown world of women's fashion. If that's what they wore, that's what they wore. "Sir, this is why we need to create some sort of warning mark. The ladies shouldn't go beyond for their own safety."

She twitched as if struck. "No, that is not what we need."

Miss O'Connor's inability to allow the men to protect her scorched his nerves. "If not that, then I can see the need to post extra lifeguards at all times."

"Are you completely out of your mind? Women are not cattle to be guarded from rustlers."

"Can you be any less practical?"

"My goodness, but your creativity astounds me." Miss O'Connor stepped around him as if he was inconsequential, and her tone stung with reprimand. How did he think she was a child? "Truly, don't you think there's another way?"

Then she turned her back on him. Unthinkable for a civilized lady toward her betters. Did she just accuse him of being an imbecile? "Excuse me." Irritation seethed between his teeth.

As she peeked over her shoulder, a hint of a smile tipped the corner of her mouth. "Of course." She blinked innocently as if she meant it, and then addressed Charles Broadwater. "I think the best opportunity we have for the safety of women from here on out would be to adopt the new swimming costumes European women are wearing. That does away with all this excess fabric dragging a person under."

Mrs. Broadwater gasped. "But modesty, Charles, we must protect the modesty of our patrons."

"I wore a much less bulky swim outfit at college, Mrs. Broadwater." She reached a hand out and took the lady's in hers. "I assure you, modesty was not compromised. However, we could swim with safety. Wouldn't that be a suitable compromise?"

The colonel stroked his manicured goatee as he thought. Then, putting a hand on his daughter's head, he said, "Miss O'Connor, would you be able to show us some of these new designs? If Mrs. Broadwater and I could take a look at them, I'd consider replacing all the rental costumes. But we still have the challenge of affordability."

The frizzy little Rapunzel tossed a conqueror's grin at Hugh. The sparkle in her amber eyes seared him like a burning beam swinging from a roof to bowl him over. An odd thought snuck up on him. If he had to work with her, he'd have to protect himself from this fiery female.

Here's a quick sample for you...
Queen of the Rockies, Book 1

*Therefore, all things whatsoever ye would that men should
do to you, do ye even so to them: for this is the law and
the prophets. — Matthew 7: 12, KJV*

HELENA, *Montana Territory — November 7, 1889*

Stop that!" Calista Blythe wrestled her skirts free from
the insistent waif. "What are you doing?" She twisted
around in a circle, as she collapsed the umbrella, dodging
packages as they tumbled. Waiting for her carriage to circle
back down Main Street, the newly erected Power Building's
massive stone walls seemed a good idea to keep her out of
the sharp wind. But Calista hadn't counted on a street
urchin to mug her. They were getting too brazen — and
desperate — with winter descending on Montana. But what

could she do about dozens of orphans dumped off of trains? Something had to be done for the abandoned children, no one adopted when they reached the last stop on the Orphan Train route. But no one did. Calista's heart squeezed a little.

The child twisted her hands into Calista's blue velvet coat and held on like a bedraggled kitten clawed into a tree trunk. "Please miss, don't let 'im whip me no more." The little girl whimpered in a heavy Irish brogue as tears ran muddy rivers on her reddened cheeks and she trembled in the cold.

"Who?" Calista craned to see around the corner of the grayish pink battered stone of the business building that served Helena, Montana's Last Chance Gulch. She caught sight of Albert Shanahan's handsome, stunned face as he endured confrontation with an angry manservant. The thin switch whistled through the air and slapped against the butler's gloved palm.

Calista's body rattled with an involuntary shudder. "Oh, my!" Calista ducked back before she drew attention as the manservant entered a nearby shop. Had the little bumpkin been whacked with that weapon? "Why are you in trouble?"

A nearby door rattled against the wind. The manservant's growling voice carried on the sharp, cold wind from a shop doorway. "If you see the little chit, you'll let me know immediately. Yes? She's been nothing but trouble since Chicago Joe purchased her indenture. Stupid Irish whelp." The bell jangled as wind mixed with a light snow forced the door closed behind him. Then his footsteps pounded on the walkway coming close.

The dirty little girl pressed against rough-cut stone of the enormous Power Block building. She hunkered down and whispered, "Please—" Her petite frame seemed like an ant against the massive structure housing multiple businesses. Helena, a city blooming with intricate pink and gray stone and brick architecture on Main Street, sprouted buildings that encompassed an entire block.

Calista pushed backward, adjusting her skirts until the child disappeared into the frills and ruffles of her blue velvet coat and day dress. From the looks of her, the material would add warmth to the quivering little body. Calista opened her reticule and pretended to search inside as the man stomped to the arced stairway.

He took a long look between the tall buildings.

She peeked between lowered lashes. Adjusting the strings and juggling the velvet purse into her overloaded basket, Calista worked to appear as one of the flustered many preparing for the festivities the next day when the president would sign Montana into the union as the 41st state.

Calista waited a few minutes before glancing after the black-suited manservant. Orphans, too long ignored and neglected, needed safety and schooling. This little one seemed to have a home, though not a safe one. Calista's heart constricted. Why did people treat other people this way?

She couldn't loiter on a busy street concealing an indentured servant all day. What if Mr. Shanahan saw her unexpected secret? What would she do with the little urchin then? Return her for a beating? Calista closed her eyes. Not if it was within her ability to stop it!

"Is he gone?" The little one poked her head around Calista's skirts, sniffled, and ran her nose along a grubby sleeve.

"I think so." She bent to meet the child's eye-level. The girl was so small and poorly dressed for the weather in a calf-length wool work smock. A light snow melted into spattering rain. The clouds broke for an occasional glimpse of sunshine, but not enough to dry the wet, muddy gulch or warm the blue-lipped child. Not enough to keep anyone from a chill without proper protection. Calista's heart squeezed. "Oh, child! Where are your shoes? Don't you have a shawl or coat?"

The girl's woolen stockings stank from the wet ground. "No, miss. I didna have time for 'em." Her Irish trill beautiful in contrast to the horror of her situation.

"You sound lovely, like a little meadowlark." Calista lifted the heavy velvet coatskirt and pulled the little girl against her warmth. As she wrapped the tiny shoulders, she couldn't feel more than skin and bones. "What's your name?" Warm soup and dry clothing would help, but she still needed to know why the child ran in fear. Had she done something terrible? Could some intervention help?

"I be Lea Murphy, miss." The heart-shaped pixie face looked up through strands of mussed brownish hair.

"Lea Murphy." Calista smiled. "How pretty your name is, and so are you under that grime."

Lea shivered and stared at her soaked feet, little toes crossing and rubbing. "I don't want to be pretty, miss."

What an unusual response. "Well, Lea, maybe you can tell me a little more about your situation."

She shook her head, but pressed closer in a shivered spasm.

"Here comes my driver. If you'll tell me why you think you're in such trouble, I'll see what I can do to help. Would you like a bowl of soup to warm up? Then we can get you home safe."

Lea's tears started again, and she sniffled. "I ca—," she hiccuped. "I canna — go home." She let out a wail that could bring back the man with the switch. As soon as the sound leapt from her throat, Lea clamped a dirty hand across her mouth.

Calista's stomach plummeted. What if that horrible man heard? She moved onto the sidewalk and glanced in both directions as if she wondered where the sound originated. He must have gone into another shop. Only the two men, Mr. Shanahan and Mr. T. C. Power, with backs to the sudden gust, remained near the bank's front steps. They didn't seem to hear anything above the wind.

Thank you, Lord. A smile lit her face as she signaled to the Blythe family driver. The sun blinked behind a cloud. "Thank you, again, Lord. Your timing is perfect."

Lea looked up at the sky. "I dinna t'ink he much listens, miss."

Calista hugged her and smiled, "I think he just did."

But Lea didn't return the smile.

The carriage splashed through a puddle and pulled to a stop alongside the nearest hitching post. Calista's driver swung down and stopped short at the sight of his mistress' skirt bundle. "Miss Blythe?"

In that moment, Calista followed the nudge in her spirit. "We have a surprise guest for lunch, Charles. Please tuck a blanket around her and pull the curtains. She's quite cold."

"A lost one, huh?" The driver spun a blanket around Lea. Not a bit of the mite could be seen, but a small sigh floated back to Calista. Charles tucked the blanket end under and slid a warmed brick beneath her feet.

A tiny head poked out of the bundle from the corner of the carriage. She could be any little girl headed home for an afternoon nap. Except for the tangled hair and dirty cheeks.

Calista climbed in beside Lea and tossed a furry robe across them both. "Home, please." What would her parents do when she brought home not only a child, but one that appeared to live in the gulch gutters?

The coach pulled away from the bank building where Mr. Shanahan's impassioned speech held Mr. T. C. Power captivated. Maybe the conversation kept them from noticing anything — unusual. Any other day, Calista would love to catch Mr. Shanahan's eye. Many of the city's debutantes thought him quite extraordinary husband material, with his congenial personality, good looks, and excellent social connections. But today...

He looked up as the carriage passed. Mr. Shanahan's blue eyes warmed her like a hot springs soak at the new natatorium as he smiled and tipped his top hat.

Calista's mouth went dry. Could he read her nervousness? She smiled with a nodded recognition and slipped the window cover in place — and waited, heart thumping hard as cattle running across hard ground. No shout. No chaos in the streets. Calista heaved a sigh as she sent up a prayer of thanks the men hadn't realized Miss Calista Blythe had just stolen someone's child!

THANK YOU FOR READING THE SAMPLE OF QUEEN of the Rockies. If you'd like to continue the story, visit AngelaBreidenbach.com for the entire series.

ABOUT THE QUEEN OF THE ROCKIES 6-BOOK series

From the Author

Celebrating romance is fun, but when I found out about how the state of Montana came to be and about the founders who lived in the newly crowned capital city, Helena, well, what better setting to tell a romantic story? The research, history, and fun! Wow, this was quite the experience for me, as an author, and I hope it is for you as the reader too!

Helena became the capital city of Montana on 30 October 1864.

Montana celebrated statehood on 08 November 1889.

QUEEN OF THE ROCKIES ~ 1889 (HELENA, MT):

Calista Blythe enters the first Miss Snowflake Pageant celebrating Montana statehood to expose the plight of street urchins. But hiding an indentured orphan could unravel Calista's reputation, and her budding romance with pageant organizer, Albert Shanahan, if her secret is revealed. Will love or law prevail?

From the Inside Flap

Albert flipped open his pocket watch. She'd be expected any second as one of the last competitors. He looked up the stairs — and there she stood. The light from the chandeliers shimmered off her gown, creating an ethereal glow that sparkled around her entire being. His heartbeat picked up speed as if a trolley ran out of control on a hill without brakes.

Calista saw Albert and rewarded him with a smile that slammed into his heart with an electric zap as if that trolley had just jumped the tracks. His feet carried him to her with a mind of their own.

"You cannot imagine how beautiful you are to me." Albert whispered.

"I —" Calista's hand fluttered to her heart.

The most beautiful time of the year in Montana is September. The weather is cool, but comfortable. The mornings are crisp and days often very sunny. The trees start changing to golden yellow. They glow! Our pines include Tamaracks that also turn yellow. I believe they're the only pine that changes colors with the seasons. If you've never heard of a Tamarack, it's also called the Larch. Really worth seeing! But you'll want to come toward the end of September for that phenomenon.

Sadly, all our hummingbirds fly south between mid-August and mid-September. The deer, both white tail and mule, get more gutsy. My garden is a constant battle with those varmints. Coyotes start to calm down, but we're still cautious of bear and mountain lions. I have to guard my last batch of Oregon grapes from the wild turkey hordes marching through. Lost them all one year in less than twenty minutes!

September is apple, squash, and the beginning of hunting season. We have delightful cider press parties, bonfires with s'mores, and the last of our farmers markets. Our Bitterroot Macintosh apples are a favorite for both cider and pie. They make fantastic jelly as well. You'll find tons of great flavors and homemade preserves in the fall all over Montana at the weekend markets.

Another thing Montana has for visitors and locals alike are festivals, concerts, and sporting events. The city of Missoula nearly shuts down for Griz football games! Tickets are usually highly sought after. Around Christmas-time, there are regular Nutcracker ballets in several cities as well as premium holiday concerts that include favorites from Celtic Women, Celtic Thunder, Mannheim Steamroller, and more. Casting Crowns were just here this summer! My husband and I buy tickets to whatever concert is in the holiday lineup for our presents to one another each year. Best date night ever!

When you come, my big tip is to check for local sporting events. If one is happening where you're visiting, be sure to book your hotel in advance. They fill up fast! Especially for school tournaments elementary through college. Our school sports are still a favorite feature of news casts. You'll hear high school through college sports reported constantly while middle school tournaments make the news in Montana. Family and community are top priority in Montana. People smile and say hello here. They'll point you in the right direction and send you to their favorite places. So please come visit Montana.

One of my "don't miss" spots is a rain forest on the west side of Glacier National Park. A rain forest, you say? Why, yes! You'll read in book six of this series, Flame of the Rockies, about the largest fire in US history. That fire changed the Pacific Northwest from a vast white pine and cedar landscape to lodgepole pines. But it didn't reach that area of what is now Glacier National Park. There's an amazing short walk through an ancient rain forest on the Trail of the Cedars. You'll wander among giant cedars, over a bridge with a gorgeous, teal-colored creek, and be able to climb into trunks of trees for photos. For more information:

HTTP://WWW.HIKINGINGLACIER.COM/TRAIL-OF-THE-CEDARS.HTM

The hike is pretty level and all ages can easily walk the less than a mile horseshoe trail. We took ages infant through eighty!

Montana is a very beautiful, civilized state even though you'll be able to find vast wild country, too. Just don't forget to watch the sunsets. Breathtaking!

DEAR READER,

I hope you enjoyed *Song of the Rockies*. I had so much fun with Mirielle and Evan, and also getting to know all the newsies. I wrote five more stories that tell what happens as Montana becomes a state in full 6-book series, *Queen of the Rockies*, that starts with book 1 of the same title.

As an author, I love feedback. Candidly, you're the reason I'll continue to explore the courageous debutantes of Helena, the Queen City of the Rockies, and a few more special places along the way. So, tell me what you liked or loved, what questions or thoughts this book brought to mind, or what made you laugh and cry. You can write to me at: angela@angelabreidenbach.com I answer emails personally. I'll also mail you an autographed bookplate for your book for free, if you email.

And please visit me on the web at: AngelaBreidenbach.com or tune into any of the podcasts like Genealogy Publishing Coach. You can find them on my website. I'd be honored to have you subscribe. Regardless, I hope you'll enjoy listening.

Finally, I need to ask a favor. If you're so inclined, I'd appreciate a review of *Song of the Rockies* from anywhere you purchased your copy. Your feedback is important to me! Reviews can be hard to come by for authors. You, the reader, have the power now to make or break a book.

Some great places to leave reviews are Bookbub, Barnes and Noble, ChristianBook.com, Goodreads, Amazon, and your own social media. Be sure to tag me (@AngBreidenbach) or email me a link where you post so I can share it out to readers who would like to hear what you have to say so they can choose their next favorite read.

Thank you so much for reading Song of the Rockies, spending time with the newsies, and I hope you'll also enjoy the sample chapter of Heart of the Rockies. I also tucked in the first chapter of Queen of the Rockies in case you didn't read that one yet, too, with a little about each book in the series, so you know what else is coming. But most of all, thank you for spending time with me. I'm honored!

Appreciatively,
Angela Breidenbach

ABOUT THE AUTHOR

Angela Breidenbach is a bestselling Montana author, genealogist, and speaker. As a Montana author it's one of her favorite places to write about, whether in an historical or contemporary setting. She's taught Muse, her fe-lion personal assistant, how to high five, shake, sit, come, lay down, rollover, and jump through a hoop. Surprisingly, Angela can also!

To ask Angela to speak for your group or event, please contact her at: angela@angelabreidenbach.com
http://www.AngelaBreidenbach.com
Facebook/Twitter/Pinterest/Instagram: @AngBreidenbach
Bookbub: https://www.bookbub.com/profile/angela-breidenbach or @AngBreidenbach